Looking Through Windows

Jack & Fran -
Thank you for your
interest in my book! I
hope it brings you a few hours
of pleasure!
Kristin

Looking Through Windows

KRISTIN CARTER ROWE

Library of Congress Control Number: 2012903565
ISBN: Hardcover   978-1-4691-7379-5
               Softcover   978-1-4691-7378-8
               Ebook   978-1-4691-7380-1

Copyedited by Ma. Chrizel Liz De los Santos
Reviewed by Miguel Paolo Pernia

This is a work of fiction. Names, characters, places and incidents either are the product of the author's imagination or are used fictitiously, and any resemblance to any actual persons, living or dead, events, or locales is entirely coincidental.

This book was printed in the United States of America.

To order additional copies of this book, contact:
Xlibris Corporation
1-888-795-4274
www.Xlibris.com
Orders@Xlibris.com
111565

For Matt, because he is my everything

Chapter 1

When we moved into that old house on Wooster Street, I had no idea that the neighborhood—as serene and quiet as it was—would absorb me so. At first, I was certain that I would not be happy there, that I would have to fake my way through each day for Willie's sake, pretending—as I always did back then—that life was wondrous and joyful and that my marriage was stable.

Sometimes I even believed it. I had become so good at playing the happy wife, at least when I had an audience, that I sometimes forgot to be sad when I was alone. Willie probably knew of my falsehoods, even at the tender age of six. But instead of confronting it, he played along, rarely showing himself without a mask or costume to change his identity. At six, he needed such accoutrements to bring his fantasies to life. But by the age of thirty-two, I had no need for such things. I was very good at hiding behind my own face.

I was also very good at watching, at losing myself in the lives of others in order to forget my own, especially on Wooster Street. I immersed myself in the daily activities of my neighbors, so much so that I became an integral part of their everyday existence. Perhaps it would be more accurate to say that I made their lives part of my own. Just as Willie changed his reality by transforming the living room into a hidden hideout for his favorite superhero of the day, I transformed the rooms of my neighbors, and all the secrets that came to life there, into my rooms and my secrets.

To the west I had the Spains to watch, Michael and his wife, Janice. The first time I saw Janice, she was standing on the back porch. It was summer. Willie had gone to camp, and I was alone in the new house for the first time since we had moved in earlier that month. It had been a long few weeks of unpacking and organizing, shopping, and putting things in their place. I had a hot mug of coffee in my hands, one that

I could actually take the time to taste, and the air smelled clean; it was warm and fresh and new.

The Spains' house was a mirror image of ours—a two-story rectangle of vinyl siding that was regularly breached by windows of various sizes on all sides. All the homes were blessed with wide front porches and shorter porches at the back. That's where we both were—on our back porches—when our eyes met over the wooden picket fence that separated our small yards; the fence was high enough to keep a child inside but not high enough to prevent a friendly shake or the passage of a cup of sugar above its pickets.

She was sitting in a rocker in the corner of the porch when I first saw her. Then she stood and walked into the sunlight, her short hair looking a bit gray in the brightness of the sun. At first she only smiled, even more so when I smiled back. It seemed to surprise her when I lifted my hand and offered a friendly wave. "Beautiful day, isn't it?" I said, trying to start up a conversation.

Her eyes squinted in the sun, and she tilted her head slightly. "Yes, it is." She stared at me for a moment and then took a few steps closer to the edge of the porch nearest me.

"You just moved in?" she asked. She was now at the end of her porch, so I walked to the end of mine. We stood only twelve feet or so apart.

"Yes. I'm Charlotte," I offered, waving slightly. I did not tell her my last name. It was too embarrassing.

"Janice Spain," she offered back. "But please call me Jannie." She paused only briefly, surveying my face and never losing eye contact. It was a bit unnerving to be analyzed so obviously, yet she seemed so kind that I took no real offense. "Are you new to the area?"

"We just moved here from Boston. My husband wanted to get out of the city."

She smiled, her eyes no longer squinting in the sun. "And you?" she asked.

"Excuse me?"

"Did you want to get out of the city too?"

"Oh, yes. My son will be starting first grade after the summer. I think the suburbs will be good for him."

Jannie nodded as if she understood, and took a noticeable breath. She looked out across the yard, which had recently been mowed, and eyed the flowers in the well-tended beds along the back fence. "My sons are all grown up now," she said. "But I remember when they were Willie's age. It seems like yesterday." She turned and immediately registered the perplexed look on my face. "I met your son a few days ago. That's how I know his name. He's a very nice boy."

I nodded and sipped the warm coffee. "So it's just you and your husband in the house now?" I asked, though I knew full well the answer.

"I'm around here a lot," she said. There was a hint of sadness in her voice. "But I don't live here anymore." She paused and filled her lungs again with the morning air. "I left my husband last winter."

"Oh, I'm sorry."

"Don't be sorry," she assured me. "It was time for me to go. We both knew it. We're still close in many ways . . . always will be."

"Well, that's good. I mean, it's nice that you could part on such friendly terms."

"I wouldn't have had it any other way, not after twenty-seven years of marriage." A slight breeze blew past, and she closed her eyes as it touched her face.

"Wow. That's a long time to be married. It must have been difficult for you to leave."

She stared into the yard for a long time before saying, "I come by less and less as time goes on. Mike isn't adjusting as well to the separation as I had hoped."

I nodded as if I understood. "So you're not actually divorced?" I asked, immediately regretting my intrusiveness.

"No." She pulled her hands up and folded them gently against her chest. "He doesn't actually know I'm here this morning," she said, turning back to me. "I know it's a lot to ask, but I'd appreciate it if you didn't mention that we spoke. I think he'd be upset that he missed me and . . ." She looked down momentarily, and I sensed she was fighting to hold something back. She tilted her head slightly. Our eyes met again. "And he would probably be very upset that his new neighbor knows so much about his private life already. He's a very private man, always has been." She sighed deeply. "I'm sure he'd be upset with me for telling you about our situation."

"Oh, don't worry," I assured her. "I won't mention any of it."

Jannie smiled. "Thank you," she said sweetly. "I better go now."

As she started across the porch to the back door, I called to her. "It was nice to meet you," I said, waving.

She turned briefly and waved back with a faint smile. Then, without a further word, she headed back inside and disappeared from view.

Chapter 2

That same night at dinner, I thought about telling Robert of my conversation with Jannie. But after we sat down and I saw that familiar look in his face—that distant, worn look—I chose not to. Jannie was too kind—too nice and new—to share with him. He would tarnish her somehow and certainly find fault with her for leaving her husband after so many years. I liked her despite the brevity of our encounter, and I feared he would ruin her for me. I chose to focus on Willie and his first day of summer camp.

"Willie, tell your dad and I about the wonderful things you did at camp today."

Willie sighed. "Mom, I already told you a thousand gazillion times."

"But you didn't tell your dad. I'm sure he wants to know."

"What's that?" Robert asked distractedly, looking up from his nearly empty plate. He had barely spoken since we sat down, his mind still at work while he chewed and swallowed.

"I was asking Willie to tell you about camp. Today was his first day."

"Charlotte," he grunted, scooping up the last of his peas and potatoes with his fork. "I hope you didn't register him as 'Willie' when you signed him up for camp. His name is William. Willie Webb sounds ridiculous."

I stabbed at my chicken. I hated chicken. *Certainly not as ridiculous as Charlotte Webb*, I thought to myself.

"William, tell me about your day," he continued. "And get that silly mask off your head at the dinner table."

Willie slowly pulled the mask off the top of his head, where it had been resting throughout the meal. "We just played and stuff," he grumbled.

Robert lifted his brow. "That 'stuff' is costing me a fortune, so I'd appreciate a little more detail than that."

Willie glanced at me, and I urged him to continue with a suggestive tilt of my head. Then I forced down the last piece of chicken and stood up. As Willie struggled his way through a slow recitation of the day's events, I preoccupied myself with the dishes in the sink.

Robert's plate was empty now, and he pushed it toward me as I returned to the table. As always, I took it without comment along with the remnants of dinner—dirty napkins, silverware, stained plates, and a nearly empty butter dish. I left the salt and pepper in the center of the table, where they always remained as silent witnesses to the dysfunctions of our household.

"Willie, why don't you go take a shower," I suggested after he cleaned his plate.

"But, Mom," he immediately complained. "Can't I watch TV first?"

"Go take your shower, William," Robert commanded, pointing his finger toward the open archway.

Willie grumbled as he stood up noisily and stomped out of the kitchen. After he left, I tried to connect with Robert. I always tried. Sometimes it worked. Increasingly, it did not.

"There's a movie on at nine o'clock. We could make some popcorn, pour a few—"

"I can't," he interrupted, showing no regard for the excitement I had forced into my words. "I'm going back to the office for a few hours. I need to get ready for a court conference in the morning."

Robert was still working for the same law firm as he had in Boston. He had been given the task of opening a satellite office in Brickwell, a city that was steadily growing and predicted to be an important center of commercial and technological activity in the coming years. By accepting the assignment, Robert had gotten his partnership offer and a hefty bonus. I got to move into a sixty-five-year-old house over a hundred miles from my family and friends. Then there was Willie, who got the best things of all: a house filled with lots of rooms and mystery, a neighborhood filled with kids (though none of them lived next door), and a new school surrounded by lots of green grass and trees.

It's not that I felt cheated, not completely. At least I had windows, lots and lots of windows, that offered glimpses into the lives of my neighbors, neighbors who were less than twenty feet away on both sides, neighbors whose lives were much more mysterious and deeper than my own. Every day I thanked God for two things: my precious Willie and my windows.

Robert made his way through the open archway, leaving me to stand dejectedly by myself in the kitchen. I heard him cross through the front rooms and then up the stairs to the second floor. I looked up at the ceiling and felt the storm of his footsteps as he made his way into our bedroom. Willie was taking his shower downstairs, and I could hear the gentle spray of water in the distance. There was a loud thud each time he dropped the bar of soap.

I stood motionless and listened for a long time to Robert's feet shuffling across the floor above. Even though he was in our bedroom toward the front of the house and I was in the kitchen at the back, I could hear him clearly. I tried, for reasons that still baffle me, to imagine his expression as he changed into more comfortable clothes and refreshed himself in the bathroom.

I don't know how long I stood there before my focus switched from imagining Robert's expression to the realization that the ceiling needed a fresh coat of paint. The white had faded into an ugly gray. It disturbed me how easily the gray must have overwhelmed the white. I imagine it crept in slowly, barely noticeable at first, and then erased away the cleanliness of the white while no one was looking. What was once new and fresh and inviting was now old and drab, something to be avoided until a stroke of paint could take it away. If only life could be so easily cleansed.

Chapter 3

*R*obert left just as I tucked Willie into bed, his small desk lamp still lit so that he could flip through his stack of comic books. After I kissed Willie good-night, I poured a glass of red wine and sat down with it on the front porch. It was a warm, clear night.

Wooster Street was an old street, dating back to the 1930s. It was narrower than it should have been, which meant that cars were forced to travel slowly or else risk sideswiping one of the many other vehicles parked along the curbs. Trees lined the street on both sides, standing so tall and wide that their branches touched high into the sky, leaving little room for a glimpse at the stars. The trees too had been around for decades. Their roots often peeked out from beneath the sidewalk squares, making it difficult for some of the older people to walk on the uneven surface. The kids, however, loved the bumps and dips, and they could often be seen racing down the sidewalks on their dirt bikes, their front tires beating hard against jagged edges of cement and the errant roots that lurched in between.

Tonight it was quiet. Most of the kids were already tucked into bed, worn and tired after a long day in the summer sun. I could hear voices from the porch of another house up the street and could see the flicker of citronella candles on several across the way. I sat in my Adirondack chair, the one my mother had given me as a housewarming gift, and sipped at the warm, dry wine.

To my left, on the western side, was the Spains' house. The front porch light was on, but the front living room was dark. I stood up, walked over to the edge of the porch, and looked back along the side of the house. I could make out a faint glimmer of light through one of the windows toward the back. The light flickered. Perhaps someone was watching television. It had to be Jannie's estranged husband, Michael.

I hadn't yet met Michael Spain. In fact, I had only caught quick glimpses of him through the windows. Based on what Jannie had said, I suspected he was a lonely man, a lonely man who was now watching television by himself in a big dark house.

I walked across the front porch and peered over at the house on the other side. One of the neighbors down the street had told me that a young single woman in her thirties had recently moved in. I hadn't seen her yet despite repeated efforts. I wasn't even quite sure she was living in the house because it was empty during the day and only the porch lights came on at night. I suspected they were on timers.

As I peered over the rod-iron railing that ran along the front porch, I saw nothing but darkness beyond the glimmer of the front light. It was going to be another dull night, another night by myself, another night to perseverate on the cruel incompleteness of my life. At least that's what I thought. The prospects of the night changed when the red Corvette arrived about ten minutes later.

At first, I felt anger when I saw the car. It had driven too fast down the street, narrowly missing a few parked cars. My thoughts instantly flashed to Willie. Every time I witnessed a threat to his safety, I felt outrage and fear. Sometimes it could stay with me all day, irrationally interfering with any other thoughts. Other times, like now, it was fleeting, a momentary sear of pain and worry.

When I saw the strange driver rush around the back of the car to open the passenger door, my interest overcame my anger. That's when I saw her for the first time. She eased out of the seat, her hand outstretched to grab hold of the man's hand as he assisted her to a standing position and then gently kissed her cheek. She looked up at me as I stood on the porch gawking, and my face reddened in the darkness. She smiled briefly in my direction and then let him escort her into the house with his hand around her waist. I watched for the lights to go on, but they never did.

She seemed, through the dimly lit darkness, to be a beautiful and mysterious woman, a woman certain to have interesting stories to tell. I promised myself that I would get to know her better if she ever showed herself at daylight.

After I had finished my wine, I sat for a few more moments and enjoyed the serenity of the night. When my eyes became heavy and the passage of time had dulled my thoughts, I rose from the chair, took a last look at the red Corvette and the darkened house, and slowly made my way back inside.

I crossed through the front living room, picking up one of Willie's red capes that he had left on the floor. As I entered the family room through the curved archway, I passed by the large bay window and looked out. My curtains were still open, and I had a direct view into the Spains' family room next door. My curiosity piqued, and I neared the window, careful to stand to one side so as not to be caught snooping. Through the sheer curtains that hung in their oversized window, I could just make out the shape of two figures sitting on the couch. The television was still on.

I strained to get a better look, still partially hiding behind the folds of curtain that hung down the side of the window. Unable to see clearly enough because of the glare from the table lamp behind me, which reflected off the window, I reached back and turned it off. The room went black and gave me the courage to press my face closer to the glass. After my eyes adjusted and I became suspicious that it was Michael and Jannie sitting on the couch, I looked at my watch. It was nearly ten o'clock. Had she stayed next door all day? Or had she left after we spoke this morning and came back again, suffering from the same loneliness as her husband? And why would they break up after so many years of marriage anyway? Was he abusive? Had he cheated on her?

As I pondered these thoughts, I watched the two silent figures next door. They sat side by side, not a word seeming to pass between them. The television set caused strange, episodic streaks of light to flash against their faces, bringing them at once into view and then quickly out again. After many long minutes, without any significant movement or happenings, I pulled myself away from the window and headed upstairs, intrigued by Jannie's nighttime visit and full of questions.

As I crossed the upstairs hall and approached the master bedroom, I saw my reflection in the full-length mirror that hung on the wall to the left of the bedroom door. It caused me to pause, and then it caused me pain.

When I had married Robert eight years earlier, I weighed 125 pounds. At five feet six, I was slender and fit. Now, at the age of thirty-two, after two miscarriages and the miracle birth of a 9.5-pound son, I weighed 160 pounds. I always blamed my weight on my pregnancies, but the truth was that I never made it past the first trimester with my first two; and though

Willie was a large baby, the math simply did not work. The truth was that while I could blame some of the 35 pounds of weight gain on fertility pills and pregnancies, the bulk of it was attributable to three forces that had entered my life at various stages of my marriage: stress, depression, and lethargy. Of course, as with most evils, these forces directed me to the three dark places: the refrigerator, the pantry, and the couch.

As I stood there, pondering my figure and all the unnecessary food that had shaped it, I recalled the "gift" Robert had given me for Mother's Day. I walked back across the hall to the spare bedroom, the one on the eastern side of the second floor. It was right next to Willie's room, and I peeked in on him from the doorway. His head was half covered by his comforter, and I could see the pile of comic books on the floor below his dangling hand. It made me smile to see him sleep so peacefully, so happy and unaware of how uneventful life could become.

I stood outside Willie's doorway for only a moment before I entered the spare room and saw my "gift." The ominous structure stood silently in the dark. I approached it, not bothering to flip on the light.

When I had first seen the treadmill, I was flabbergasted. Initially, I had been surprised that Robert had even remembered Mother's Day and then stunned that he had bothered to buy me a gift. But when I saw that he had given me a piece of fitness equipment, I realized the game that was in play. I realized that the "gift" he had bothered to purchase was less for me than it was for him. It would have been different had I asked for it or had I already been on a fitness quest. But truth be told, until the moment that I first saw the treadmill, I didn't even realize how heavy and unfit I had become. But since that day, every look I took at myself was a hard look, a hard and painful one.

I had not yet used the treadmill despite Robert's consistent reminders of its existence. I feared that if I stood upon the belt and let the motor force my feet into motion that I would be putting something else in motion as well—my fate as the second-in-command of my own life, with Robert as my captain. But now, as I stood in the dark with that mirror image still clear in my mind, I wondered if my resistance was well-placed.

I did not dwell on the thought for too long because my focus was suddenly interrupted by loud bangs and voices coming from next door. I rushed to the side window, which had not yet been draped, and looked down toward my neighbor's backyard below. It was not the Spains' backyard, which was on the opposite side, but my other neighbor's, the one with the boyfriend in a Corvette, the one who never put on her inside lights at night.

I could not see her, but I could certainly hear her. She screamed and yelled in a language that sounded like Italian. Several items, one of which looked like a shovel, whizzed from the back of the house and onto the grassy yard. From the direction of the projectiles, I guessed that she was standing on the back porch. I did not see the man again, but I heard the back gate slam and his footsteps as he apparently ran down the driveway on the opposite side of the strange woman's house. Then I heard the Corvette speed away, sounding even faster than when it had come.

I stared into the darkness, able only to see what was lit or shadowed by her back porch light. She soon appeared on the lawn, collecting the treasures she had so easily and ably thrown. As she started back toward the house, a small shovel and some other unidentifiable shape in her hand, I swore I heard her laughing.

She reached the first step leading to the porch. That's when she stopped and looked up, her eyes directly in line with my own. I abruptly stepped back, believing her to have seen me, and knocked my back sharply against the control panel of the treadmill. My back ached, and my heart raced. How could she possibly have seen me in the darkness? After a few tense moments, I leaned forward and slowly eased my head toward the window for another look. I feared she would still be there, looking up at me with an accusatory finger. But she was gone. All that remained was the glimmer of the back porch light and the strange shadows it cast about the lawn.

Chapter 4

Robert arrived home after I went to bed that night, and he was already on his way out the door when Willie and I came downstairs the next morning.

"I might be late tonight," he said, not bothering to break his stride as he headed for the front door. "There's a lot going on at the office."

From the family room, I silently watched him leave and then turned to Willie. "Go eat your breakfast. We have about ten minutes before we have to leave for camp."

Willie was wearing one of his superhero masks and the cape that I had picked up from the floor the night before. "Can I try to eat with this on?" he asked, pointing his finger at the plastic mask. There was a tiny hole where the mouth had been painted on.

"I don't think the cereal will fit through that small opening, do you?" I asked. A thought then popped into my head. Maybe I should wear the mask. If I could make my mouth that small, it would certainly limit what I could eat.

"What's so funny?" Willie quizzed me as he pushed the mask up to his forehead. There was a smear of toothpaste under his nose, and I reached over to wipe it off.

"Nothing, just one of those adult things," I explained as I wiped his face clean.

"You have a lot of those," Willie groaned and then made his way into the kitchen.

I followed him, habitually looking out the kitchen window as I passed. Michael Spain was already seated at his own breakfast table with a newspaper in hand, his back to me. Jannie was nowhere to be seen.

"Did you meet the woman from next door?" I asked as I reached for a packet of oatmeal and began preparing it.

"What?" Willie mumbled. He was reading the back of the cereal box.

"I met the woman next door yesterday, and she said she met you." I popped the bowl into the microwave and hit the start button.

"Oh yeah," he said distractedly.

"Did you talk to her at all?" I asked, curious about what they might have discussed.

"Not really." He shrugged. "I think she's a witch or something."

"Willie!" I scolded him, fully aware of his tendency to exaggerate. "That's not very nice."

"But it's true," he persisted, his nose still pushed up close to the back of the box.

"Why would you say that?"

"I dunno. Can I order one of these magic rocks?" he asked, his voice now lifting with excitement.

I dropped Willie off at camp, made a quick run to the grocery store, and then hurried back to the house. I was anxious to see if the Italian woman was home.

It took several trips out to the driveway to bring in all the grocery bags. My driveway ran along the Italian woman's fence, which was less than ten feet from the side of her house. Because her own driveway was on the opposite side, I had a direct view of her house and yard and, more importantly, an opportunity to peek into her windows as I walked back and forth. All I caught were a few glimpses of furniture, including two plastic chairs on the back porch and a chaise lounge in the yard. No one seemed to be home.

Disappointed, I climbed the stairs to the back porch for the last time, a plastic bag of groceries in each hand, and looked yet again over at the Spains. There was no one in the yard or on the back porch. *This is going to be a dull summer,* I thought.

I often wonder now what I would have done had I known then all of my neighbors' secrets, the ones I would soon discover. Would I have done anything differently? Would I have been scared away? Would I have left that house on Wooster Street?

Chapter 5

The morning was uneventful. I put away the groceries, made the beds, cleaned up after Willie, and did the laundry. I even stared at the treadmill for a solid five minutes before walking out of the spare room and closing the door behind me.

When lunch came, I made myself a sandwich, grabbed a soda, and headed onto the back porch to enjoy the sunshine for the first time since I had dropped Willie off. That's when I finally met him.

Michael Spain had also chosen the back porch to sit and eat. He was looking in my direction as I made my way through the screen door. I tripped on the old welcome mat the prior owners had left at the house and nearly dropped the paper plate that held my sandwich. After I regained my balance and straightened up, he nodded to acknowledge my existence. Since his nod was more than I had gotten from my own husband earlier, I took it as an invitation for conversation.

"Beautiful day, isn't it?" I yelled over, realizing at once that I had said the exact same thing to his estranged wife the morning before.

"Not bad," he said with a noticeable absence of joy. He was an attractive man, the sort of man who would normally garner attention if it were not for the look of displeasure that dominated his face. It was not quite a scowl, but it was definitely more than a frown. He was an unhappy man. There was no hiding that.

"I'm Charlotte. We just moved in."

Again he nodded, forcing a slight smile to form on his lips. "Welcome."

No wonder she left, I thought. *He's not much of a conversationalist.*

He pulled up his wrist and glanced at his watch. I ignored his indifference and fought for some adult conversation.

"Are you home for lunch?" I asked, now walking across my porch toward his.

He pulled up his sandwich and looked at it. His eyes returned to me, and he nodded again. "Yes."

"Do you work nearby?"

He started to stand. "At the college."

"Are you a professor?" I asked, but he was already headed back inside. He did not answer my question, but he did lift his hand in a small effort to wave good-bye, the door closing quickly behind him.

"It was nice to meet you!" I yelled, even though I liked his wife a whole lot more.

I stayed outside for another ten minutes, glancing over at every small sound I heard to see if he was coming back outside. He did not.

I resigned myself to another dull afternoon of soap operas and housework. Thoughts of getting a job repeatedly surfaced in my head, as a job would get me out of the house and allow me to meet other people, adult people, people who would talk to me, people who might actually use the electricity in their houses. But Willie had to come first, and Robert would never allow it. He had made that very clear before Willie was even born.

"If we're going to have children," he had said sternly, "then I want you to stop working. My mother worked all day long when I was a kid, and I hated it. I won't have my children raised the same way."

Truth be told, I hadn't given him any resistance. I wanted to be a full-time mother. The thought of leaving Willie in the hands of another woman made my stomach go sour. But now, as he was getting older, I felt the need for more. The big question, the one I could not completely answer, was, more of what?

I sat down on the couch to fold clothes and began to watch my soap opera. On the first set of commercials, I went to the laundry room and shifted a load of clothes into the dryer. It was stuffy in the small room, so I opened the window, which looked out onto my driveway. That's when I heard a phone ringing. At first I thought it was my own phone, but when I turned away from the window, I realized the ringing was coming from my neighbor's house.

The ringing persisted for quite some time before it stopped. Then I heard her voice. I could not see her despite my efforts, and I could not make out what she was saying. Some of her words were not spoken in English.

I stood by the window for several minutes trying to listen to her conversation before the screaming started. There were words I did not understand but several of them I knew quite well, words that one did not usually hear coming from a neighbor's window. Most neighbors would have shut their windows if they had planned on saying such things or if they had caught themselves losing control, but not mine. She screamed a number of profanities without apparent care for who could hear before I heard the squeaking sound. It was a violent, repetitive squeak as if she was rubbing wire against wood. It persisted for several short seconds. Then there was the *thud, thud, thud* of something against the wall and then a louder thud, followed quickly by the sound of a bell and a crashing noise.

There was a slight moment of silence as I strained to see what was going on. Then, without warning, I saw something quickly propelled onto the back lawn. I couldn't make out what it was, so I rushed out of the laundry room and down the back hall that opened into the kitchen. I abruptly stopped my momentum, slowly pushed open the screen door, and then inched my way onto the back porch, making sure I didn't trip on the welcome mat again.

As soon as I was outside, I had a clear view of her back porch and part of her yard, but I did not see her or the unknown object that had been thrown so violently onto the grass. I waited a moment and listened, half expecting—and definitely hoping—to hear her voice again. Except for the sound of a car passing by in the street out front and the occasional chirp of a bird, there was only silence. No more Italian. No more profanity. I decided to get a closer look.

I walked cautiously down my back steps, trying desperately not to make any noise. I crossed the small patio of fieldstone and approached the gate that led into my driveway. It squeaked as I opened it, and I made a mental note to get lubricating oil at my first opportunity. I paused again as I stood in the driveway and looked toward the street. I wanted to appear uninterested if she happened to be watching from some hidden spot.

My curiosity continued to grow at a rapid rate. I found myself obsessed with discovering what she had thrown into the yard in anger. After much internal debate while I stood so nonchalantly in my driveway, I approached her fence on the opposite side. Once there, I bent down as if to pull a weed, hoping I might be able to see through the pickets. I could not, at least not very well. Finally, I stood up and simply looked over the top of her fence, my stomach aching with the fear of being caught.

There it was, its cord and plastic strewn about the lawn like a victim of a tragic battle. She had ripped the old-fashioned rotary telephone out of the wall and had chucked it—in all its glory—onto the grass.

I was so mesmerized by the sight that I did not see her approach the back door. "Did I scare you?" she called out to me. A wrenching scream erupted from deep inside, and I instinctively grabbed at my chest. My heart skipped a beat.

She slowly opened her back screen door and walked out onto the porch. She did not wait for me to answer. I couldn't speak anyway. There was a numbing thud in my ears, and my throat had constricted to the size of the mouth hole in Willie's mask. "I hated that phone anyway," she said, a slight smile evident on her lips. It was a smile that would haunt me throughout the next few months of our relationship.

She did not have a strong accent, which struck me as odd given the scene I had witnessed and overheard the night before. There was a detectable difference in how she spoke her words, however, and her appearance was stunning. She was at least five feet eight, with dark olive skin and long, flowing chestnut hair. She was wearing open-toed heels and a miniskirt, with a tank top that accentuated a very curvy and full figure.

"I'm sorry," I said, barely speaking above a whisper. "I thought I heard something."

She briefly glanced toward my open window, her lips still in a slight smile. Then, with one of her hands grasping at a post that held the roof on the porch, she said, "I'm Isabella."

I shyly responded in kind, "Charlotte."

"Just like the spider in the book," she gently teased, and my heart sank. "I'm sorry about the noise," she continued. "Would you like to visit?" She spoke so fast, barely pausing between words, that it took me a moment to fully register her question.

"Okay," I heard myself say. There was no gate from my driveway into her backyard, and I hesitated, unsure how to get through.

"You'll have to walk around the front. I'll meet you back here," she said. She then quickly disappeared inside her house. I walked all the way around and found her waiting for me at the back end of her driveway, two large glasses of something red in her hand.

"Strawberry daiquiris," she explained as she handed me one of the glasses. "It's a good thing you came by, or I'd have to drink it all by myself.

I bet you could use this as much as me." She winked as if she knew a secret, something about me that no one else knew, maybe not even me.

I really didn't want to drink alcohol so early in the day, especially since I had to leave soon to pick up Willie, but I didn't want to lose out on the opportunity for something interesting. She motioned me to one of the plastic chairs on her back porch, and I obediently sat down.

She sipped at her daiquiri before speaking again. "Don't be afraid of me," she said. "I tend to get emotional at times. I find that if I just let it all out, it doesn't hurt so much later. It's just my nature."

"What got you so angry?" I asked, sipping slowly at the icy drink.

"Who. Not a *what* but a *who*." Her voice went flat, and for a moment I was certain she would flare up again, maybe spit out fire and smoke. She was certainly capable of it, of that I was already certain. But she didn't spit anything, choosing instead to take another sip of her drink.

"That guy from last night?" I persisted, looking up at her only briefly before plunging the straw back into my mouth. I drank too quickly, and the inside of my forehead turned to ice.

"Carlos? You saw that too?" She laughed, not casually but with full joy. "Oh, you must think I'm insane. No. No. No. It wasn't him. He wouldn't dare call me again."

Before I could prod further, the other phone—the one she hadn't yet killed—rang in the distance. Her eyes narrowed, but she did not stand up. I watched her carefully as she tried to preoccupy herself with her drink. It wasn't working this time. Each time the phone rang, her lips tightened and her eyes turned a darker shade of brown.

"Do you want me to get it?" I asked cautiously.

"No." Her voice was steady and defiant. "Let it ring."

It did ring, and it kept ringing at least six more times before I asked, "Don't you have an answering machine?"

She sucked more of the frozen daiquiri up the slender straw. "Never have. Never will. She'd leave her goddamn squeaky voice on it every day. I'd either go crazy or my head would explode." Her anger was brewing, and she tried to joke it away. "One day you'd see smoke coming out of my windows, and when you came over to see what it was, all you'd find would be a pair of my high-heeled shoes in a pile of ash. The world would know that God had decided I'd had enough, lit me up like a pile of kindling, and saved me from her hellish ranting."

"Her?" I continued to sip at my daiquiri.

"Yes. The devil herself." She eyed me for a moment as if trying to decide what to reveal. Perhaps she was undecided whether I was worthy of her tale. Whatever her hesitancy, she finally leaned forward and then, as she stood, abruptly said, "My husband's whore."

I nearly choked. "You're married?" I managed to ask, my heart aflutter with anticipation.

She stood on the porch and looked aimlessly toward the sky. It was a beautiful summer day. "I used to be," she whispered. A slight wind caused her hair to stroke against her face.

"Divorced?"

She laughed, mostly to herself, and then shook her head as if it still surprised and amused her. "Widowed."

"Oh, I'm sorry," I immediately apologized, feeling once again that my intrusiveness was becoming an uncontrollable evil.

"Don't be sorry, honey. It's just as well. That bastard would never have given me a divorce." She turned now and smiled again. The ringing had finally stopped.

"How about you? You're married, right?"

"Yes," I said. "My husband's name is Robert. We just moved here."

"He must work a lot," she said. "I haven't seen him around much."

"He's a lawyer, so he works a lot of hours."

She smiled at me, and I suddenly felt uncomfortable. "A lawyer, huh?" she said. "Maybe I should be apologizing to you."

I laughed with her though I didn't quite get the joke. We sat there a bit longer and finished our drinks. Then, before I could think of anything else to say, she stood and said, "I suppose I better get back inside. Thanks for sharing a drink with me. We'll have to do it again, Charlotte."

I was sitting on the edge of the plastic chair, my empty glass held loosely in my hand, wanting desperately to question her further. How did her husband die? And if her husband was dead, then why was his lover—his whore—still calling her? I tried to garner the courage to ask her about it, but the courage never came. It would have to wait until another time, perhaps the next time she decided to throw something onto the lawn.

"It was nice to meet you, Isabella," I said somewhat naively and then headed back toward my own rectangle of insanity.

Chapter 6

There was definitely something amiss on Wooster Street. Everyone's marriage was ended or ending. Even I was on the verge of a marital breakdown, though I didn't have the courage to fully admit that to myself.

"I met our neighbors today," I told Robert at dinner that night. He had come home earlier than usual, once again appearing tired and ornery.

"Which side?" he asked, showing no real interest in the subject.

"Both actually." He did not look up from the paper or his half-empty plate. I continued anyway. "I met Michael Spain first. He wasn't very talkative. Nothing like his wife."

"She's a witch, Dad," Willie piped in, his mouth filled with potatoes.

"What?" Robert asked, suddenly showing some interest.

"Willie!" I scolded. "I told you to stop that."

"Why do you think she's a witch, William?" Robert put down the paper and folded his hands on the table. I picked up his plate and listened for Willie's answer, slightly angered that Robert had given an ear to his remark.

"Because I saw her from my bedroom window. She was sitting on the roof. She was just sitting there and looking at the sky. Probably she was casting a spell or something. She must have flown up there on a broom because there was no ladder or anything for her to climb on. And she wasn't wearing a cape." As Willie told his story, he continued to fork mashed potatoes into his mouth.

"William, don't talk with food in your mouth," Robert scolded.

"What do you mean she was on the roof?" I asked, surprised that he hadn't mentioned anything about the matter to me and stunned that a woman her age—she had to be in her late forties or early fifties—would do such a thing. I walked over to the kitchen window and looked up.

There was no one on the roof, of course, and I didn't see any way to access it from the second floor. Was there a ladder or an entry on the other side?

"She was just sitting up there," Willie answered, shrugging his shoulders as if he didn't understand my question.

"William, is this another of your stories?" Robert asked, his tone stern and serious.

"No, Dad. She was sitting up there. I swear."

I looked out the window again, searching for an explanation of how she could access the peak.

Willie grabbed hold of his empty plate and stood up. "There was no ladder, Mom. She flew up on her broom. I know it."

Robert shook his head. "What are they teaching this boy at that camp?" he complained. "Or maybe it's those damn costumes he's always running around in. I told you that this play acting—whatever the hell you call it—is not right for a boy his age."

Willie immediately defended himself. "Dad, I'm telling the truth. She was sitting—"

"Enough, William!" Robert stood up and approached his son. "I don't want you making up any more stories, and I certainly hope you don't act this way with your friends. Charlotte, I want you to put an end to those costumes."

"No, Dad!" Willie cried. "I'm telling the truth!"

"I don't think he's lying, Robert. Maybe there's a way to access the roof from the other side."

"Oh, for Christ's sake, Charlotte. Don't encourage the boy." Robert gave us each a look of disgust and walked from the room. I wanted to scream at him, just like Isabella had screamed at Carlos and the alleged whore, but I couldn't do that in front of Willie. I hated it when Robert looked at me like that, like I was smaller than he was, like I was dim-witted and could be reminded of my inferiority with a simple but mean-spirited grimace. That degrading smirk was meant to belittle me, but it was the fact that he did it in front of Willie that made it especially painful this time.

Willie had tears in his eyes. "I really saw her up there, Mom. Is Dad gonna take away my costumes?" His mouth twisted into a thin, crooked line at the painful possibility that his most cherished belongings might be taken from him. *How could Robert be so cruel? Even if Willie was telling a fib, it was relatively harmless.*

"You won't lose your costumes, Willie," I assured him, running my fingers gently through his dark brown hair. His equally brown eyes were wide and full of fear as I leaned over and kissed his forehead. "Besides, I believe you. Next time I see Jannie, I'll clear things up with her, okay?"

"Okay," he whispered. "But be careful."

Willie headed into the family room and clicked on the television. "Only for a few minutes, Willie," I called to him. "You still have to take your shower."

He didn't answer me. All I heard were the voices from the television. I looked up and closed my eyes, praying that Robert would stay upstairs for a while. I didn't want another scene with Willie. I didn't want to receive that look again. I didn't want Willie to see how weak I had become.

I never did get to tell Robert about Isabella that night. It was just as well. When he did finally meet her a few days later, there was an immediate and mutual dislike between them.

Chapter 7

As the weeks passed, I rarely saw Michael Spain outside of his house. He was gone during the day, and when he would arrive home in the late afternoon, he would hurry into his house and lock himself away from the outside world. As for Jannie, I would see her occasionally in the house, sitting next to Michael on the couch or at the kitchen table. They didn't seem to talk much. After all those years together, they were probably comfortable in the quiet of each other's company.

At least I had gotten better acquainted with Isabella. "Do you know if the guy that lives on the other side of me is a college professor?" I asked her one night when we were sitting on the front porch, sharing a bottle of red wine. Robert continued to work odd hours, and Isabella would often give me the pleasure of her company after Willie made his way to bed.

"I don't know. Why, is he cute?" She lifted her eyes suggestively.

"I wouldn't know," I said. "I've been off the market too long."

"Oh, you're not off the market, honey." She laughed. "You're just harder to get, that's all."

"That's not why I'm asking," I assured her, but I couldn't help but smile. When she was with me, she was always happy and laughing, nothing like the woman who screamed in Italian almost every time she picked up the phone. "I thought he worked at the college, but if that's true, then why doesn't he have the summer off?"

"Why do you care so much about what this man does?"

"I don't know. I've only spoken to him once, but the whole situation over there is so strange." I leaned forward in my chair and looked over at the Spains' house. It was dark inside again, only the flicker of the television noticeable in the side window. That's how it always was.

"What's so strange?" She stood up and walked over to the side of the porch nearest the Spains' house. "Does he have wild parties?"

"No. That's probably the furthest thing from his mind."

Isabella eyed me for a moment and then asked, "Well, what's the big secret then? What's so strange about your *other* neighbors?"

I had promised Jannie that I wouldn't tell Michael about our conversation that day or about her visit, but I hadn't promised my silence with regard to anyone else. *Should I tell Isabella?*

"Charlotte," she taunted me, returning to her seat. "I do think you are keeping a secret. Let's have it, girl."

"Look who's complaining about secrets," I said. I was stalling, but the truth was that the mysteries of her life, the details she kept so carefully hidden from me despite our many conversations over the past few weeks, had become troublesome.

"What do you mean?" Isabella's tone was playful, but there was a quick flash in her eyes. I had seen that same flash of emotion every time the forbidden topic came up, but I had not yet deciphered its meaning. It wasn't full-fledged anger and not quite sorrow, but still it unnerved me, and I hesitated long enough for her to prod me further. "Charlotte?" she asked.

I eyed her momentarily. "My point is that you have many more secrets than I do, Isabella."

"Oh you think so?" she queried, still smiling, still hiding behind her beauty.

"Well, you still haven't told me about your husband."

"What is there to know? He was a shit who liked to fuck—other women, of course." She raised her glass, high enough that the light from the moon, which barely squeaked its way through the highest branches of the trees, sparkled off the rim. She stared at the red wine against the background of thick branches and leaves, dark and ominous as they were along the dimly lit street. "Here's to Anthony, my late husband. May his overly active body lie painfully still in the cold earth."

"Isabella!" Even though I hadn't been to church in years, not since Willie was a toddler, her comments made me cringe in anticipation of the lightning strike from the heavens above, that place that I still whispered to at night when my soul felt lost and alone.

Isabella continued, ignoring me. Despite her fiery words, she spoke in a calm and tempered manner. "And let's not forget his whore. May she too soon find her way to the grave. At least before she has the time to make another goddamned phone call." She gently lifted the wineglass and placed the rim against her painted and parted lips, quickly swallowing the remaining liquid inside. When she had completed her dramatic show, which was really more for her own entertainment than for mine, she glanced at me sideways. "I'll make you a deal."

"I think you've had too much wine," I whispered.

"You tell me your secret about the handsome professor," she continued, "and I'll tell you one secret about my husband's death."

The air was still. For several seconds, it seemed that the only sound on Wooster Street was the melodic creaking of a cricket from beneath the wooden planks of the front porch. "You go first," I insisted.

She pursed her lips as she pondered my suggestion and then tilted her head sideways, her chestnut hair falling gracefully against her right shoulder. "Want to know why the whore keeps calling me?"

I nodded.

She hesitated slightly. It was then that I first caught sight of her pain. It was brief, hidden deep, and suppressed, but I saw it for a moment, that flash in her eyes. That flash of sorrow was a hint of her struggle to maintain, to survive. "Because she thinks that I killed Anthony."

"What? Why does she think that?"

Isabella gulped in the fresh air, filled her lungs, and then emptied them in a slow and deliberate manner. As soon as the last breath escaped her, she clicked her tongue, snapping back to the feisty, bright neighbor I had become so infatuated with. "No. No. No. I said one secret and that was it. Now out with yours."

"You're kidding, right?"

"A deal's a deal, Charlotte." She poured herself another glass of wine from the bottle that still sat on the porch beside her chair. "And it better be good."

What was I to believe about this strange and beautiful woman? I was oddly pulled to her, yet she frightened me in a way I couldn't yet comprehend. She was that kind of person, full of life and full of secrets, beautiful but capable of ugliness, honest to the point of being painful yet false in so many ways as well. She was everything, not all of it good and not all of it bad. Above all, she was interesting, and I was at a point in my life when I craved whatever was offered to me outside the mundane realities of my own existence.

"Well?" Isabella complained, raising her perfectly plucked brows. She was radiating now as if her slight, ambiguous confession had rejuvenated her spirit. Her expression was, as usual, inexplicable, and for a moment I thought she might actually be insane. It was a thought that had crossed my mind more than once.

I did not want to tell her about Jannie, not now, not knowing she might be capable of the worst of all sins. It's not that I believed her guilty based simply on the apparent beliefs of her husband's mistress, who seemed to call often to remind Isabella of her suspicions. It was that I could not rule out the possibility of her guilt, however slight it might be. Frankly, I did not yet know Isabella well enough to appreciate what she was capable of, beyond loud outbursts of vulgarities and occasional pitchings into the yard.

But then again, can we ever know anyone well enough to define the limits of their anger or the ends to which it can bring them? I doubted that. I too was an angry person. It was anger born of loneliness and neglect, marital neglect like Isabella's. As I sat there thinking about her situation, I realized something, something that stunned me into telling her about Jannie. I realized that I did not even know myself well enough to define the limits of what I could be capable of if pushed too far. If I confirmed my own suspicions about Robert and his late-night work sessions, what would I do? What was I capable of? I had no idea. I didn't think I could hurt another person, not even Robert, whom I still loved despite his increasing absences and his painful glare. So I told Isabella what she wanted to know. I had no right to be judgmental.

"I'm afraid my secret is a lot less interesting than yours," I said, unable to find a better word than *interesting* to explain her revelation. "I met Michael's wife the first week I moved in. She was out in the backyard. We didn't talk very long, but she told me that she had left him after twenty-seven years of marriage."

"Did she say why?" Isabella asked. "Did he cheat on her?"

"She didn't say, but somehow I don't think that's it. She still cares for him. She even stops by to see him. I got the impression that he's having a hard time dealing with it and that her guilt brings her back to make sure he's okay. I see her next door sometimes, a lot actually."

"Doing what?"

"Watching TV with him. Sitting with him at the breakfast table. Nothing spectacular."

"Have you talked to her recently?" Isabella pressed.

"No. I haven't had the chance. I haven't seen her outside. Although . . ."

"What?" Isabella turned the chair, its wooden legs creaking against the porch floor, and pulled herself closer.

I leaned forward and whispered, my voice cracking in amusement. "Willie has spoken to her and thinks she's a witch. He claims he saw her sitting on the roof one day."

Isabella scoffed, but she too couldn't help but smile again. "Poor Charlotte."

"What?"

"Well, on one side of you lives a witch who sits on her roof, and on the other side of you is me. And God knows what I am . . . besides crazy."

Chapter 8

I had run out of milk and bread and was in desperate need of tampons (or stamp-ons, as Willie called them), so I went directly to the grocery store after I picked Willie up from camp. I actually enjoyed shopping with Willie, just the two of us trekking down the aisles, him in search of food with villains or superheroes on their labels and me in search of something that I could cook for dinner besides chicken. Willie was wearing another mask. He had pulled it out of his backpack when he climbed in the car from camp and prided over his workmanship in its creation. I told him he could wear it in the store so long as he didn't scare any of the little children (the only color on the mask besides disturbing shades of gray and black was red, which Willie used to form little droplets of blood at the corners of the mouth he had cut into it).

"Why do you need those, Mom?" Willie asked as I grabbed a box from a shelf in the personal hygiene section.

I placed the box gently at the bottom of the cart so that I could hide it beneath a load of groceries. "You're too young to understand. I'll tell you when you're thirteen."

"Last time you said you'd tell me when I was twelve." He looked up at me, but all I could see were his pupils through the small holes he had cut out of the mask for his eyes.

"We'll see," I whispered, pulling out my shopping list.

"That's what you said, Mom." He was standing on the cart as I pushed, and I could feel his weight fighting against me.

"Why don't you walk, Willie. You're getting too heavy to push on this thing."

"I'll walk if you tell me about the stamp-ons," he offered, and I swore I could see a devilish smile beneath the blood-dripping mouth of his mask.

34

"Willie," I warned, lifting my eyes as I always did when I was on the brink of doling out a punishment.

"Okay. Okay," he grumbled, stepping down from the back of the metal cart but still hanging on with his hand as he walked. We turned the corner and headed into the next aisle. "Hey, isn't that the guy who lives next door?"

I looked up and saw Michael Spain analyzing the paper products. He pulled a large bag of napkins off the shelf and continued on his way in front of us. He had not heard Willie and had apparently not seen either of us.

"Is it him, Mom?" Willie whispered to me, somehow knowing he should keep his voice low despite his customary habit of speaking too loud and saying too much.

I nodded and kept pushing the cart, intent on following my neighbor until I had an opportunity to introduce myself again. He moved quickly, like he didn't want to be in public too long. I found myself racing to keep him in sight.

"Why don't you say hi," Willie offered innocently.

"I will," I whispered as if he were my confidante. In many ways, he was. My little six-year-old boy was one of the best friends I had.

It was then that Willie took it upon himself to make a move. He had always been confident in himself, so different than me in that way, and that made it easy for him to make friends. So when he ran ahead and stood between Michael Spain and the shelf of jelly jars, his ugly mask still covering his face, it was not all that surprising to me.

"I'm Willie," he said innocently and then pointed to me. "We live next door."

Michael Spain looked up at me briefly and nodded. Then he slowly bent down and neared the eyeholes Willie had cut into his mask. "Is that a boy in there or a hideous monster?"

Willie laughed, sliding the mask up to his forehead. His dark hair flowed up and under the top of the mask, causing little wisps to spring out haphazardly as he talked. "A boy," he said excitedly, "but when I put the mask on, I become a man with superpowers."

"Are they good or evil powers?" Michael indulged him.

"Mostly good, unless I decide I don't want to be."

That was the first time I heard Michael Spain laugh. It was short-lived, but it brightened his face, changing him for a moment from a lonely man to a somewhat handsome professor. I immediately dismissed the thought and said, "We met the other day."

"Charlotte," he said evenly, allowing the smile to fade away. "Michael Spain," he offered and extended his hand, giving me a firm shake when I reached out. He was all-business with me but not with my son.

"So what brings you to the grocery store, Willie?" he asked, returning to the safer world of my six-year-old.

"My mother needed stamp-ons," he said innocently, pointing to the box that still remained exposed in the cart. I felt my soul lift and die on the dirty aisle floor.

Michael Spain let out an unexpected laugh. "Well," he said, choking on his words, "those are important."

"My mother won't tell me what they are until I'm twelve or thirteen."

"Oh my god," I whispered as I pulled my hands up to my reddened face. Willie stood there, his mask pushed up against his forehead, tufts of hair now sneaking out from behind the papier-mâché. He was looking up at our new neighbor with anticipation, hopeful that the secret would finally be revealed.

To my great relief, Michael simply said, "That's what my mother said too."

"Willie," I interrupted before he could push the issue, "why don't we let Mr. Spain finish his shopping."

Michael straightened up. "It was nice to meet you, Willie," he said, extending his hand. Willie reached out and shook it. "That's a good, strong handshake."

"My dad taught me how," Willie said flatly. "But I like how my mom does it better."

Michael looked at me again, his eyes asking the question that his mouth did not.

"Show him, Mom," Willie insisted, coming over to me and tugging my hand off the cart. "See, we do it like this." Willie put my hand in his, and we did our secret handshake. A firm grip, a twist into an upward hand lock as if we might wrestle, a firm grip again, a release of our hands, a snap of our fingers, and then a banging of his knuckles against mine.

Michael eyed me curiously, but I could not read him. He spoke only to Willie. "That's pretty cool."

"Yeah, it's our secret handshake. We do it every night when I go to bed, and then we do it in the morning right before I go to camp." Willie smiled. It gave me great joy that he still spoke of me with love and pride in his heart.

"It was nice seeing you again, Mr. Spain," I said. He seemed so much like the professors I had in college, so much older in appearance than in years.

"It's Michael," he said, his face still flat but not as stern as it had been on the porch that day. I had cracked his facade, if only just a little.

"Okay," I said softly and pushed my cart past his.

"Bye, Michael," Willie waved as we passed.

"Bye, Willie. It was a pleasure."

Chapter 9

I stared at the treadmill for a long time before I actually plugged it in. Then I stood on the belt and fiddled with the fancy buttons for a few minutes before I turned it on. I started slowly at first, unaccustomed to the movement, and worked my way to a fast-paced walk. Walking would have to do for now. At 160 pounds, I just didn't have the desire or the knees to run.

I angled the treadmill so that I was looking out the window toward Isabella's house. I hadn't heard her scream in a few days, nor had I seen her yet today. I was beginning to wonder what she was up to. It was nearing 9:00 p.m., yet there was no movement in the house. Darkness was arriving as the sun began to set on the horizon. I had checked her driveway several times during the day, but her car was gone. She had a garage, and it was possible she had parked inside, but I doubted it. She never used the garage. Nor did we, at least not now when the weather was so warm.

I didn't know what Isabella did during the day, but she was usually out. She told me she worked downtown at a salon, cutting hair and painting nails, but I had my suspicions. For one, she refused to cut Willie's hair when I had asked her, even though I offered to pay, claiming she didn't like to cut children's hair. When I then suggested she cut mine, she scoffed again, something about not mixing business with friendships. It was all very suspicious.

So I started paying attention to when she left the house and when she returned. I was pretty good at keeping tabs on her, but there were days when she would not leave the house at all and other times when she would be gone for several days. When I asked her once about where she had gone during one of her multiple-day absences, she told me she had been visiting relatives in New York. I didn't believe her, but I never told her that.

I had thought about following her, about trailing her one morning when she left the house. But although I was interested and intrigued by my neighbor, I wasn't quite ready to go that far. It was bad enough that I spent so much time thinking about her secret life, the one she would not reveal to me no matter how much wine she drank on my front porch.

Isabella was mysterious, careful not to reveal too much about her whereabouts and deep thoughts. But when she was home, she did not try to hide herself from view. Her curtains were rarely drawn, and more than once I had come upon her undressing with no regard for her open windows. She was a showgirl, a drama queen, and she knew how to entertain even when she wasn't quite sure who was watching.

As I walked on the treadmill, my heart racing after only a few minutes, I realized how well I could see through Isabella's second floor windows. I had a particularly good view of the rear bedroom, which she had converted into something of a yoga studio. There were several carefully placed mirrors along the wall opposite me and a large rubber mat on the floor (I had seen her carry it into the room). I had seen her in this room before, stretching and rolling and meditating. If there was ever someone in need of meditation, of calmness, it was Isabella.

I was so focused on the yoga room that I didn't hear the sound of the front doorbell above the purring motor and the noisy thud of my heavy feet against the rolling rubber mat. In fact, had I not seen the two policemen walking down my driveway in the fading light, I would never have known they had come to my lonely house on Wooster Street. The instant I saw them, I turned off the treadmill and watched through the window.

It was when they reached my back gate and swung it open that it dawned on me to go downstairs. I peeked in on Willie as I crossed the hall. Finding him fast asleep, I walked softly down the wooden stairs to the first floor. The officers were already knocking on the back door as I approached the kitchen.

I flicked on the back porch light, and they showed me their badges. Neither of them cracked a smile as they sized me up and took darting peeks into my house.

"I'm Officer Johnson," the more heavyset man said. "And this is Officer Lucarelli." He nodded to the younger man behind him, a fit, handsome man with a less hardened look on his face. "Do you know the lady who lives next door?"

I knew he was talking about Isabella because he nodded toward her house as he spoke. There was something about him that I didn't like. Maybe it was his tone when he said her name. "Yes," I said. "Is there something wrong?"

He ignored my question. "Have you seen her today?"

"No." I stood in the open doorway with the warm night breathing against my body, wondering whether I should ask them to come in. Instead, I said as little as possible. I unexpectedly felt the need to protect Isabella.

"When's the last time you saw her?" he asked, his voice still official and unapologetic despite the late hour. The man behind him, the handsome one, only listened.

"I saw her last night." My tone was cautious, and the seasoned officer picked up on it instantly.

"Are the two of you friends?" he asked, trying to force some gentleness into his question.

"Can you tell me what this is about?" I asked. I prayed for a simple, uneventful answer.

"We'd just like to talk to her. It's nothing serious." He was a decent liar, but his younger counterpart betrayed him by momentarily lowering his eyes when I glanced his way.

"Did she do something wrong?" I asked.

"We're not at liberty to say, but it's important that we speak to her." He held out his large hand and handed me a card with his name and number. His fingers were worn and dry, and his nails needed serious manicuring. I pictured him biting down on his fingers as he sat in his patrol car. "Please call us if you see her. It's for her own good."

I took the card, but I said nothing.

"Can I have your name, ma'am?" he asked, still official but not quite impolite.

"Charlotte," I said softly.

"And your last name?" He held a small white pad in his hand and had scribbled down my first name. He looked up at me curiously when I hesitated. "Ma'am?"

"Webb. It's Webb," I whispered. My name didn't incite any humorous comment from him about the famous book so similar in name, but the younger man, the silent one who seemed much gentler and less affected by the stresses of the job, smiled at me and winked as if he understood the irony. Poor Charlotte Webb. While the spider in the book could save a pig, she couldn't even save herself.

I waited until the officers had left my backyard and were no longer visible before shutting the back door. I thought about calling Isabella, but I knew it would be a wasted effort. She wasn't home. I hadn't seen her there all day. Besides, she was unlikely to answer the phone even if she had been in the house.

I ran to the front room and looked out the window facing the front porch. The two policemen were getting back into their cruiser. The young man was laughing, and I suddenly felt very stupid and insecure. Was he laughing about my name? Or had he noticed the silly running shorts I had donned for my brief "workout"?

It was dark outside now, but I could make out the shapes of their heads as they sat parked on Wooster Street. They weren't leaving. They were waiting to see if she would come home. The larger man, the one with the unattractive nail beds and sandpaper hands, lit up a cigarette. The smoke lifted in the darkness and dissipated out the top of the open window.

I was still standing by my front window when I heard the back door creak. "Robert?" I called, but there was no answer. I could hear the sound of someone walking across the floor and knew instantly that someone was in my kitchen or maybe in the hall that ran alongside it to the east (Isabella's side, as I called it). My stomach suddenly felt empty and unstable, but I couldn't move. I listened. I listened and heard the feet move slowly in my direction.

I peeked over my left shoulder through the front window and saw the patrolmen still sitting in their car. I was readying myself to dash for the door when I heard her voice. "Charlotte," she whispered from the back of the house. "It's me, Isabella."

"Jesus!" I said, pulling my hands to my chest in relief. "You scared the shit out of me!"

"Shhh!" she said, as she crept out of the darkness, careful to stay clear of the windows. "Are they still out there?"

"Yes. Their car is right out front. What's going on?" I motioned her into the back hallway where we would be safe from interested eyes.

Once inside the narrow walls and hidden from view, Isabella seemed to relax. She leaned against the wall and took a deep, cleansing breath. "I so hope you have a bottle of wine," she said dramatically, running her fingers through her dark hair.

"Are you going to tell me why the police are looking for you?" I asked, incredulous that she was so calm.

"It's nothing really," she said, tilting her head and smiling with her eyes.

"Isabella, you better tell me right now, or I'm going to tell those policemen that you're here." I looked at her sternly, but I didn't feel real anger. Oddly, I was excited—pleased, actually—that the night had turned out better than I had expected. I could only pray that she hadn't killed someone. That would have truly ruined it for me.

"Why are you being so serious?" she scoffed, stretching her arms toward the ceiling to rid a kink from her back. "You know, it wasn't easy getting over your back fence."

"Were you in the backyard that whole time?" I asked, momentarily sidetracked.

"Oh no," she said. "I was on my way home when I saw the police car, so I drove a few blocks and parked behind the elementary school. Then I walked back here and cut through the yard behind you. When I saw the police at your back door, I just waited until they left. You know you really should lock your doors at night."

"You're going to give me advice?" I complained.

"So how about that wine? My head is swimming!" She cupped her head with her hands, her red-painted fingernails framing the flawless skin of her high cheekbones. I couldn't tell whether she was frightened or excited.

"What have you done, Isabella? Why are you hiding from the police?" The words came out rushed and anxious. "You can't hide from these guys forever, you know. They know who you are and where you live."

"My goodness, Charlotte, don't get so excited. I told you it was nothing." She started for the kitchen. "Is the wine in the pantry?"

"You should leave," I said. It was bad enough that Robert treated me as a child, as an ignorant with no ability to understand the world as he did. But now, my friend, my only real friend in this boring community that Robert had dropped me into, was discounting me, ignoring my questions and sidetracking me with her words, just like I did with Willie when I didn't want to address his curiosities.

"Charlotte," she started to protest.

"I'm not kidding! Just go home!" I pointed toward the door, my anger brimming, my mind racing with insane thoughts about what she might have done. Had she slain another cheating man?

"All right," she said, gesturing for me to quiet down. Then she smiled and grabbed my hands in hers. "It's about time you let yourself lose it a little. There's hope for you yet." She gently squeezed my hands and whispered her confession, "I went to the whore's house."

Before I could respond in any meaningful way, I heard a car pull into the driveway. "Oh no, Robert's home," I whispered.

She let go of my hands. "Fuck!"

"What should we do?" I asked, suddenly less sure of myself. "He might see the police outside and wonder what's going on."

"Go watch through the side window and see if they talk to him," she instructed, and I immediately raced into the bathroom. Isabella followed me. I could feel her behind my back as I peeked into the driveway and watched Robert get out of his car.

"Why did he have to pick tonight to come home early," she whispered.

"It's after nine o'clock. I wouldn't exactly call that early," I whispered back.

"We're talking about Robbie time, Charlotte. He almost never comes home before you're in bed."

I chose to ignore the hidden message behind her remarks and watched as Robert eyed the police cruiser and then grabbed his briefcase from the rear seat. He walked down the driveway, glancing back over his shoulder for another long look, and then entered the rear yard.

I quickly turned, knocking into Isabella. "Oooh," she whined as my elbow cut into one of her oversized breasts.

"Sorry," I whispered. "What should I do? Do you want to hide in the back room until he goes upstairs?"

Isabella paused and then threw up her hands. "No. This is crazy. I'll take my chances with Robbie. I'm going to have to speak with the police anyway. I just need to think a little first."

"You didn't kill her, did you?" I asked nervously just as Robert opened the back door.

She looked deep into my eyes and gently held my face. "No, Charlotte. I didn't kill her." She eyed me momentarily and then quickly cocked her head. "At least not yet."

"Charlotte," Robert called as he walked into the family room. Isabella and I had already rushed over to the couch, where we were pretending to have a discussion. "I didn't know you had company." His eyes went directly to Isabella's breasts before he looked up and smiled at her. "Hello, Isabella."

Robert didn't like Isabella. He had made that known to me from the start. But he did like to look at her, particularly at her noticeable chest.

"Hello, Robert," she said, emphasizing the last letter in his name. "Late night at work?"

"Do you know why there's a police cruiser out front?" he asked, looking at me for the first time since he had entered the room. I wanted to push him for an answer to Isabella's question, one she had asked with a tone filled with knowledge, but I didn't. My momentary loss of control was over.

"I don't know," I lied. "It's not the first time they've parked there at night."

"It's not?" he asked, his eyes quickly flirting back to Isabella's protruding shirt. She didn't seem to notice. She was too busy looking at me with curious surprise.

"Oh no. I see them there all the time. They probably just use that spot to take their break."

Robert shrugged, quickly bored by the topic. "I'm going upstairs. It's been a long day."

Isabella started to stay something, but I warned her into silence with my eyes. "There's some lasagna in the refrigerator if you're hungry," I said.

Isabella openly frowned, her disappointment evident. Robert was equally disappointed in me, but for many other reasons. "I ate earlier," he grunted as he headed for the stairway.

"Oh, do they have a cafeteria where you work?" Isabella asked, falsely lifting her voice.

Robert stopped and turned, giving her the same disdainful look I was accustomed to. Her games were not lost on him, but he responded calmly anyway, "No, but there's a deli within walking distance."

"What did you have? Anything good?"

I couldn't believe her brazenness. She was egging him on, challenging his veracity, while two policemen sat outside staking out her house.

"A turkey club," he said, lowering his eyes for one last look. "Am I free to go now?"

Isabella shrugged and turned back toward me. I caught Robert's glare before he headed up the stairs.

"What was that all about?" I asked when he was out of sight.

"You let him off too easy. You don't ask any questions about why he's so late and then you offer him lasagna." She shook her head.

"He's a lawyer, Isabella. He works a lot of hours."

"Have you ever called the office to see if he's really there?"

"Marriage is about trust, Isabella."

She laughed loudly. "That's exactly what Anthony would say to me whenever I questioned him about his whereabouts. And we all know how trustworthy he turned out to be."

"What did you do to her, Isabella?" I asked quietly, shifting toward her on the couch and leaning forward.

"Don't worry. I didn't hurt her. Not in any physical sense."

"Then why are the police here?"

"If I tell you, will you get me a glass of wine?" She fell back against the couch and eyed me sadly.

I nodded, fearing what she would say.

"I committed a technical assault, I believe," she started, lifting her arms and shrugging as if she did not understand why her actions should warrant any labeling or sanction.

"Did you hit her?"

"No. But I did attack the thing she cherishes most." With that, she sat back up, wiped a few stray hairs from her face, and smirked. "I killed her telephone."

"What?"

"I pounded that damn contraption with a hammer." She mimicked the violent motions of her hand hammering away at an invisible phone and then sighed. "I think that was my mistake. The hammer, I mean. That might get me into some trouble. You should have heard her scream."

"How did you get into her house?" I asked.

"I walked in," she said, lifting her shoulders as if to signal the absurdity of my question. "She's a whore. She always leaves her door open to strangers."

I flashed my eyes at her, recalling her earlier warning about not locking my door at night. Isabella smiled. "Oh, Charlotte, I don't think you're a whore, at least not with anyone else's husband."

Before I could fully register the insult, she continued, "I couldn't take her phone calls anymore, Charlotte. She was driving me crazy. Besides, I already killed one of *my* phones. It was only fair that one of hers should die as well."

"Did you bring the hammer with you?" I asked, aware of the consequences she might face if she brought a potentially lethal weapon into the whore's home with malicious intent. There was a time when Robert actually talked to me about his work, so I knew a few things.

Isabella pouted. Her lips were painted perfectly. "Would that be a bad thing?"

"Oh god," I moaned. "You broke into her home with a weapon. That's got to be bad. Did you ever threaten her with it?"

"Would that be a bad thing too?" Isabella's lips remained pursed as she waited for my response.

"Oh yes, it would." I sighed.

"I never touched her, Charlotte. Even though I wanted to. I could feel the desire burning in my belly. Oh how I wanted to take that hammer and strike her in the goddamn mouth. That would have shut her up!"

"Shhh," I said, lifting my finger to my lips. "You're going to have to face the police sooner or later. Please be calm when you do, and please don't tell them anything about what you *want* to do to this woman."

"The whore, Charlotte. She is not a woman."

"Do you want Robert to help you? He can counsel you before—"

"No. No way," Isabella said quickly. "I already have a lawyer."

"You do?"

"Yes, I do. I had to get one when the whore first started accusing me of killing Anthony. The cops got real snoopy because of her."

"Does your lawyer know about tonight?"

"Not yet," she whispered as she started to rise. "I'll have to call him soon though. Can I have that glass of wine first?"

Chapter 10

Isabella stayed at my house until the cops finally left around midnight. I was surprised they stayed so long. After all, Isabella had only killed a phone. True, she had illegally entered the whore's home with a hammer and threatened her with it. Then there was the complication of her being a potential suspect in her husband's murder. But as far as I knew, Isabella had never been arrested or charged in Anthony's death, and according to Isabella, it had been several months since the fire that took his life.

As soon as the cops drove away, Isabella pulled out her cell phone and called her lawyer. I heard the sound of her voice from the back room, where she had gone to talk in private, but I couldn't pick out more than a word or two. She spoke for a brief period, maybe ten minutes or so, before she reentered the family room.

"I'm going home now, Charlotte. Ralph's going to meet with me and then drive me to the station so I can turn myself in and beg for mercy." She rolled her eyes as she spoke, but the power in her presence was gone. Reality had stolen her confidence.

"Is Ralph your lawyer?"

"Yes. He's sweet. Somewhat unattractive, but strong." She fiddled with her shirt as if her appearance needed improving.

"What did he say?"

"He's going to argue that the whore instigated the whole thing. She's been calling me constantly with her ugly accusations and threats. Hopefully, he can get me off with a slap on the wrist. I've never been arrested before, so that should help. He said something about a conditional discharge. I'm not sure what that means exactly."

I had heard the phrase before. Robert didn't do much criminal work unless it involved a current client charged with a white-collar crime, but he had once helped out a friend of his who had gotten into a bar fight.

I remembered him talking about the case and agreeing to a similar plea. "It means you'll have to go on probation and stay out of trouble for a while."

"Something like that. And I'll have to pay a fine, and I might even have to pay for her to get a new goddamn phone." She shook her head, disgusted by the idea.

"It's better than breaking and entering or assault and battery," I suggested.

"Well, I'm not out of the woods yet. Let's just hope Ralph can frighten her enough into not pushing this. He's going to get a restraining order to stop the phone calls and to keep her away from me. And he's going to threaten her with a harassment charge if she fights against the plea."

Isabella looked defeated now. She was finally realizing the foolishness of her actions. By lashing out, she had put herself in the position of being at the mercy of the one person she hated most. She looked at me with sad eyes. "Learn from this, Charlotte."

"You mean to watch my temper?"

"No, I mean to watch your husband. One whore can cause a lifetime of misery."

Chapter 11

The morning found Willie and I eating breakfast alone, as usual. Robert had paused in the kitchen just long enough to grab a mug of coffee, give me a quick kiss on the cheek—which stunned me as highly unusual—and touch the top of Willie's head with instructions for him to behave and act respectable at camp. Willie grinned and nodded, but something in his expression led me to believe that even my young son understood his father's lack of respectability. I tried not to dwell on that realization.

It was another bright morning, and I started toward the back windows to close the shades so Willie could eat his cereal in softer light. The small roof over the back porch didn't always provide much relief from the sun. As I started to pull the shades down, the ones that had been there when we arrived and that I desperately needed to update, I pressed close to the glass. First, I looked toward Isabella's yard. I was dying to learn how things had turned out for her at the police station. Unfortunately, I couldn't see much from the back kitchen window, only her fence and a little of the yard beyond its pickets. I could not even tell if her car was parked in the driveway on the opposite side of the house.

Earlier, I had looked at her house from the upstairs hall window, but I hadn't seen anything, not even a bathroom light. If Isabella was home, which I suspected she was, she certainly had no need to be up at such an early hour. And even if she did work at the salon, as she had told me, I doubted she worked any early morning shifts. Isabella did not strike me as an early riser.

Out of habit, my eyes trailed to the Spains' backyard. I could actually see more of their back porch because it was closer. Our back porches were less than twenty feet apart, separated only by the aging four-foot picket fence.

I didn't see her at first. She was sitting in a rocker in the corner, hidden partly by the shade that had been cast by the roof. I caught sight of her just as I was pulling away. She was alone. Michael had probably left for the college already. Unlike Isabella, he always seemed to be out of the house early.

"Willie," I said quietly, "I'm going to get the newspaper. I'll be right back." I started for the back door.

"Why are you going that way?" he asked. "The newspaper's out front."

I hesitated only briefly. "I need to pull the trash out first. It's trash day."

"But Daddy already did it," he said, never once turning his eyes away from the back of the cereal box. "I heard him pulling the barrel down the driveway."

"I want to make sure he didn't miss anything." I opened the back door and went out onto the porch. It was already hot at seven in the morning. I walked to the back rail and looked into my own yard before I turned to her and feigned surprise. "Hi, Jannie," I yelled over.

She turned to me slowly and then stood from the rocker. She appeared to be such a happy woman for someone going through the tragedy of a divorce. "Hello, Charlotte," she said. I was surprised that she remembered my name.

"I haven't seen you in a while," I said. "How have you been?"

She continued to smile. "Oh, I've been good. And yourself?"

"Busy. Busy." I was lying, but it was the only thing that came to mind. "You know how it is."

"Oh yes," she said gracefully. "My sons were always running around from here to there. How is Willie anyway?"

I thought of what Willie had said, about how he had called her a witch because he had seen her on the roof. "He's great. He's still going to camp and loving it."

She nodded but remained quiet. It always made me uncomfortable when people did that. It made me wonder what they were thinking behind their nods that they didn't feel comfortable saying out loud.

"How is Michael holding up?" I asked.

"Fine. Just fine." She paused again while she looked toward the sun. Then she said, "I understand he met your son. I think he got a kick out of him."

This time it was me who nodded. All I could think of were the stamp-ons. Had he told her about that? Of course he had. "Yeah, Willie can certainly make anyone laugh." I had barely gotten the words out of my mouth when I saw Willie out of the corner of my eye. He was standing in the doorway, his face pressed against the screen, no doubt trying to get a look at the witch from a safe vantage point.

"Speaking of the devil," I said and then opened the screen. "Come on out, Willie, and say hi to Mrs. Spain." I stuttered her name a little, unsure what to call her in the circumstances. Willie took a step back and shook his head. There was an odd look on his face. I lowered my voice and warned him, "Willie, don't be rude."

Jannie seemed to understand and gently yelled to him, "It's okay, Willie. I won't bite. I already had breakfast."

Willie pouted at me and then took a hesitant step forward. His curiosity was like mine. It sometimes made him do things that his internal voice told him not to do. He walked slowly onto the porch, lifting his hand slightly to acknowledge her with a small and cautious wave.

"He's not usually so shy," I said, surprised by his unusual behavior. Willie was an outgoing child, with no real fear of adults. Yet he seemed frightened by Jannie.

"It's good to see you again, Willie," she said kindly. "I think I might have scared you last time we met."

Willie remained quiet and shied up against me. "Why's that?" I asked, thrilled that she had brought it up.

"Your son caught me doing something I shouldn't have been doing," she started, taking a step closer. Willie pulled closer. "He saw me up on the roof, I believe."

Willie crinkled his nose and then looked up at me to make sure I had heard Jannie's confession. "I told you," he whispered.

"What were you doing up there?" I asked, looking up toward her roofline and wondering how she could have reached it.

"Michael was having some work done on the roof and asked me to come over and supervise. Anyway, I wanted so desperately to see the view from up there that I begged the workers to let me come up on their equipment. They resisted, but I finally won them over. It was a glorious sight."

I thought back. I had no memory of any workers on her roof. Perhaps they were working on the other side and I just couldn't see them. "I'm surprised they let you go up. That's awfully dangerous, isn't it?"

"I suppose it wasn't the wisest thing to do. I'm sorry if I scared you, Willie. I must have looked quite silly sitting up there by myself."

Willie eyed her curiously. "If you were Superwoman, you could fly, and you wouldn't have to sit on the roof to see everything."

Jannie laughed and leaned forward, her hands pressed on the rail of the porch. "I certainly felt like Superwoman up there. I could see for miles. It was just like I was flying."

I immediately sensed danger. I knew Willie too well. "Don't you be getting any ideas, Willie," I warned. "I know you like to pretend you're Superman, but you cannot go on the roof."

"Oh no, Willie," Jannie joined in. "What I did was foolish. I'd hate for you to get hurt because of something I did."

"What was wrong with the roof anyway?" I asked.

"I don't know. Something was leaking. They patched it up, and everything's fine now." She looked toward Willie and shrugged. "I guess I won't be making any more trips up there."

"My dad didn't believe me," Willie said.

"That I was on the roof?" she asked. Her voice always rang with kindness. It was unusual how she could speak at a high enough level for us to hear her across the yard, yet she never seemed to strain her voice. Her words were always soft and melodic. Her voice reminded me of my mother's when I was a child.

"He got mad because I thought you might be a witch." Willie was back to his old self now that he had heard her confession.

"I see," she said, nodding her head again. "Your father must not believe in witches."

"No. My mom doesn't either. Are you a witch?"

"Willie!" I scolded him, but I muffled my voice. "He has a wild imagination," I yelled over to Jannie.

"That's a great thing to have, Willie," she said, still smiling.

"We better go in now. It was nice seeing you again." I waved at her as I opened the screen door and pushed Willie back inside.

Willie slouched back in his chair and thumped his foot on the ground. He often did that when he wanted my attention.

"What's the matter?" I asked, still annoyed at his behavior. Although I loved his innocence, I did not enjoy the embarrassment it sometimes caused.

"Why did you rush me inside?" he complained. "She didn't answer my question."

"Willie, Mrs. Spain is not a witch. She told you why she was on the roof."

Willie smirked and looked up at me with his big brown eyes. "Yeah, I guess. But I don't remember anyone else being up on the roof, Mom. And I watched after I saw her up there because I wanted to see her fly down."

"How *did* she get down?" I asked, curious.

Willie shrugged. "I don't know. She just kind of disappeared."

"What do you mean?" I asked.

"She was sitting up there by herself and then she was gone."

"Did she climb back down?"

Willie made a face. "No, Mom. I told you. She just disappeared."

"Well, how can that be?" I questioned him. "You must have turned away or got distracted." I pulled the gallon of milk off the table and headed toward the refrigerator.

"No, I didn't," he said defensively as I put the milk away. "And how did she know I saw her up there anyway?"

"She must have seen you," I offered, wiping the table to gather the crumbs that had dropped from Willie's toast and the milk that had spilled from his overfilled cereal bowl. "Didn't she talk to you?"

"No, Mom. She didn't see me or talk to me. I was watching her from my bedroom window, hiding behind the curtains just like you do."

Chapter 12

Robert actually made it home for dinner that night, at least physically. Mentally and emotionally, he was still elsewhere.

"How old is Isabella?" he asked as he swallowed a piece of steak.

"I'm not sure. She's around our age, I would guess. Why?" Robert didn't usually ask about Isabella, choosing instead to simply complain about her. He didn't like how she dressed (too suggestive) or how she spoke (too outspoken), and he certainly didn't like our developing friendship ("She's having a negative effect on you, Charlotte. She overpowers you in every way. I hope you don't listen to every crazy thing that comes out of her mouth").

"Is she married?" He continued to eat as he spoke, occasionally glancing at me across the table to register my expression.

"No," I said. Willie was watching us in silence, still angry that I wouldn't allow him to read his comic book at the table.

Robert must have sensed my hesitation. "Never?"

I filled my mouth with steak and shrugged ambiguously. I was not good at lying, but I knew that Robert would take a firm stance against my socializing with a potential murderess.

"I heard she was married to a local doctor but that he died earlier this year," he said, putting his fork down and slowly wiping his mouth with a napkin. He leaned back and waited for me to talk.

"He died in a house fire this past spring," I said. That was really all Isabella had told me. "I didn't know he was a doctor." I hadn't pictured her with a doctor. I'm not sure why, but it didn't seem to fit.

"How did the fire start?" He was still looking at me curiously as if he expected a confession of some sort.

"I have no idea."

"Isabella never told you?" he pressed.

"No. I just assumed it was an accident. Maybe an electrical short or something." Robert knew more than he was saying, but he was feeling me out, playing me like he would a witness. It was the longest discussion we had had in weeks.

"Did you ever ask her about it?" he continued. His chin jutted forward slightly.

"Robert, what is this all about?" I put my own fork down now and started to rise from the table. His steady glare made me uneasy. I was not used to him looking at me for so long.

"I'm curious," he said.

"I never asked her about it, and she never discussed it. All I know is that there was a fire, and he died." I wiped down the counter and the stove top and then tossed the sponge in the sink. Half of my dinner still sat on the table.

"William, you may be excused. I need to talk to your mother."

"But I'm still eating," Willie protested.

"You've had long enough to eat. Go take your shower." Robert's voice was strong and stern.

Willie looked toward me. "Can I still have dessert?"

I nodded and urged him out of the room with a shake of my head. He rose, noisily sliding back the wooden chair, and then exited.

Robert called after him. "We'll talk about that act of disrespect when you get out of the shower, William." Then, still seated, he turned toward where I stood by the sink. "Why didn't you tell me about her?" he asked.

"What about her, Robert? That she was married?"

"Well, that would have been a nice start," he grumbled, remaining in his seat. "Did you know she was a suspect?"

"She's never been charged."

"So you did know then." There was anger in his voice.

"Who told you about her?" I asked, now leaning with my back against the counter. I could feel water from the sink dampen my shirt, but I didn't move away. I felt the need to stay where I was, with the support of the counter behind me, even if it was wet. "What did you hear?"

"A lawyer in my office represents her husband's life insurance carrier."

"You were feeling me out for information on her? To help a client?" While the anger showed in my voice, I still lacked confidence in Robert's presence. I knew I could not outargue him. He was too good at it.

"Isabella is the named beneficiary under a million-dollar policy and has been trying to recover the funds."

"And?" I asked. She had never mentioned any life insurance to me, and I had never thought to ask. I suddenly felt very naive.

Robert scratched at his forehead and lifted his left brow. "The carrier determined that her husband died as a result of arson. Because Isabella is the prime suspect, they have refused to pay under the policy." He stopped talking, letting his disclosure hang in the air and eat away at my conscience.

"Why is she a suspect?" I asked.

"Because she had the most to gain. He was cheating on her, maybe even planned on leaving her. By killing him and burning down the house at the same time, she could recover under his million-dollar policy and receive another whopping sum under their homeowner's policy. Not to mention the legal fees she saved. Divorce lawyers can be pretty expensive."

I hated how he spoke, like he was the prosecutor and I was his juror, ready to be manipulated and swayed, bought and sold, wooed and enticed. "Why do they think it was arson?"

"Circumstances."

"Meaning what?"

"She had plenty of motive, and she certainly had opportunity. Not to mention that the insurance investigator, the state police, and the fire chief all agreed that it was arson."

"Based on what?"

Robert tilted his head, a knowing grimace on his face. "Based on the evidence, Charlotte."

I wanted to hit him, but I didn't have the courage. Keep it simple, I told myself. Keep it simple. "What evidence?"

Robert stood up and approached me. "You mean she didn't tell you?"

"Tell me what?"

"Well," he sighed, lifting both hands behind his head and arching his back. He let out a slight groan as he stretched out the kinks in his back and neck. "Where should I start? The fire was started in the first floor family room. Whoever started it used an accelerant, gasoline to be exact. Within minutes, the house was in flames. They found him on the floor, his body severely burned and his lungs full of carbon monoxide. By the time he realized what was going on, it was simply too late."

"Where was Isabella?" I whispered.

Robert eyed me carefully. Did he think I already knew the answer to my own question, or was he trying to figure that out? I fidgeted.

"She claims she went for a drive. That they had gotten into a fight and she left. The problem is that there is no one to corroborate her story."

"Who discovered the fire?" He was draining my confidence, and he knew it. I could see it in his eyes. That was his intent, of course. He never liked Isabella, and he wanted me to stay away from her. At first I thought it was because he truly did not like her. Then, during this first conversation about her husband's unusual death, I thought it was because he thought she was dangerous. I was wrong both times, but I wouldn't realize that for some time.

"Isabella was there, but she didn't report the fire, a neighbor did," he said, coming a step closer. He gripped the counter on each side of me, his face close enough now that I could smell the meat on his breath. I thought he might actually kiss me, but he simply said, "She never went into the house. She never tried to save him. She never called for help. She stood and watched the fire burn down that house knowing he was dying inside. Now is that the kind of woman you want to hang around with, Charlotte?"

Chapter 13

That night I had a horrible dream. It started with the doorbell. When I went to the front door, Isabella was there, and she was holding a hammer. "Is he asleep?" she asked, holding the weapon up high for me to see.

"Yes, but—" I started to say.

She interrupted me, pushing her way through the door as she spoke. "I didn't actually use a hammer on Anthony. I didn't want to leave any obvious marks."

"What are you talking about, Isabella?"

She eyed me with that strange look again. "Don't you know, Charlotte? Don't you know what must be done?"

I shook my head. Even in my sleep, the anxiety of it overwhelmed me.

"He's cheating on you, Charlotte!" She screamed at me. "Don't you know what must be done?"

"He's not—"

"Yes, he is!" she screamed again.

"I made lasagna. Would you like some?" I asked, starting toward the kitchen.

As I walked away, I heard her heavy breath. Then I heard her walking toward the front stairs. "Where are you going?" I asked, my voice unsteady.

In the background, I heard a phone ringing, but I did not try to answer it.

"To do what you don't have the guts to do," she said smiling, the phone still ringing in the distance.

She started up the stairs. Only now she didn't have the hammer. She had a red gasoline can in her hand. It was big, and she struggled to carry it. I could hear the liquid sloshing inside with each slow step she took.

"No!" I screamed. "Isabella!"

I ran toward her, screaming. When I got to the bottom of the stairs, I looked up. Willie was there. He was looking at me with his mask on, his brown eyes barely noticeable through the tiny holes. The phone stopped.

"What are you doing, Mom?" he asked innocently. "Why are you screaming?"

I was frantic. Isabella was nowhere to be seen. I started up the stairs, but my hand and arm were being pulled downward. I felt the weight tug on my fingertips. I looked down and saw it. It was the red can. I now had it in my own hands.

"What are you doing with that, Mom?"

I screamed myself awake and bolted upright.

"What the hell?" Robert said sleepily, angrily, as he too sat up quickly.

"It's okay," I said. "I just had a bad dream."

"Jesus, Charlotte," he grumbled, plopping his head back onto the pillow. "You scared the hell out of . . ." His voice drifted off, and he was sleeping again.

I got out of bed and immediately checked on Willie. After reassuring myself that he was all right, I went downstairs and looked around the first floor. It was dark and quiet, and the wooden floor was cold on my feet.

I made my way to the kitchen and opened the refrigerator, not knowing why or what, if anything, I wanted. I closed it again without taking anything from inside. I went to the kitchen table and sat down, my breath still a little heavy, my heartbeat still a little fast. *Is that why Isabella scared me? Did I fear that I was capable of the same horrors she was accused of? If Robert was cheating on me, would it anger me enough to kill him?*

Never, I thought to myself. *I could never do such a thing, no matter how angry I got.* I stood up again, tired but restless. Maybe the television would help. I went back to the dark family room and fumbled around for the clicker. Then I sat down and turned on the set. It flashed on quickly, startling me momentarily, the sudden brightness forcing my eyes into a squint.

I flipped between channels for a few minutes, the bright screen flashing in the darkness with each changed station. At first, I didn't feel any presence. I was always the one doing the watching, not the one being watched. But before long, I felt someone's eyes upon me, that uneasy feeling of being the object of someone else's unwanted attention. I turned quickly to see if Robert had come down the stairs. I expected him to be standing in the dark behind the couch, but he wasn't there. Both the family room and the living room at the front of the house were empty.

I turned back around, squinted in the semidarkness, and pressed the mute button on the clicker. I sat there in the silence and listened. *Was someone in the house? Had Isabella snuck in again?*

I could hear the ticking of the clock on the bookcase. I even heard a small squeaking noise, but it seemed more mechanical, like it came from the refrigerator, than something living. "Isabella?" I whispered, leaning forward slightly.

There was no response. I stood, leaving the television on mute, and walked back toward the kitchen, my ears tuned for any sound, however small or hidden. "Isabella, is that you?" Still, I heard nothing, nothing to reveal her presence.

Even though I called her name, I knew she was not there. I knew it was not Isabella that had warned my senses.

After a quick search of the kitchen, I went back into the family room and habitually turned to the window, the one that faced into the Spains' house. That's when I saw him. That's when I realized that, like me, Michael Spain was awake at three o'clock in the morning, wandering around in the darkness. If it hadn't been a bright night, with a full moon to shine through the windows on the opposite side of his house, I might not have seen his figure by the window. But I did. I caught a glimpse of him before he quickly pulled out of sight behind his own curtains.

I neared my window casually. I understood his need to look, his need to find someone else to entertain him through the loneliness. And I did not want to embarrass him or—God forgive me—discourage him. Perhaps I *was* becoming more like Isabella. I looked out the window unconcernedly, my eyes only scanning quickly to see if he was still there. Though I believed he was still somewhere behind the curtains, I returned to the couch as if I had never seen him and pretended to watch the television set.

I had no idea what movie was playing, only that it was in black and white. I didn't even bother to turn the volume back on. Instead, I sat and wondered if he would continue to watch me. I thought he might. How nice it would be if I knew him well enough to ask him over, to invite him in to talk, or to simply watch a movie.

It surprised me that I thought such things. After all, I was a married woman. Even if I did know him well, it probably wouldn't be appropriate to have him over at such a late—or early—hour. I laughed. Robert probably wouldn't care. Why should he? He never talked to me anymore other than to probe me for information about my friends. And he certainly didn't sit with me anymore, not even to watch television. I missed the chats we used to have, but I think I missed the quiet times even more. Those were the times we didn't need to talk to feel close, to feel the comfort of each other's presence. The quiet times used to remind me of how much love we shared, when being spatially close meant something all by itself.

Perhaps it was time to test Michael, to see how far he would go. *If he was still watching me, would he follow me outside? Would he come over to talk if he saw me sitting by myself on the back porch, less than twenty feet from his own?*

I knew that if I was the one watching him, I just might be so bold. So I stood up, turned off the television, dropped the clicker onto the couch, and walked slowly to the back door, letting the moonlight shine my way. The screen door creaked loudly when I opened it as if it was angry at me for waking it from a deep sleep. I winced, looked up at the ceiling, and listened for Robert. There was no sound of him awakening. I slipped out the door to the back porch, the screen door squeaking in protest again but less noisily as I slowly closed it shut.

I had bought two plastic Adirondack chairs for the back porch, similar to the wooden one my mother had purchased for me for the front, and I slid into the one closest to the Spains' house. I was wearing only a pair of pajama shorts and a T-shirt and felt a slight chill in the summer air. I suddenly felt very self-conscious. Was he still watching? Perhaps I should grab a robe?

If I stand up now and return to the house, he'll think I went back to bed. Then he'll certainly leave, maybe even go back to bed himself. I knew I should put something more decent on, something that would cover me better, but I dared not leave. I sat on that porch and waited for him to come and talk to me.

He never did.

Chapter 14

*I*sabella came to see me a few days later. It had taken her that long to get over the fact that she had to reimburse the whore for the damage she had done. At least she would not have to go to jail for her intrusion into the whore's house, so long as she stayed out of trouble for the next six months, so long as she didn't get arrested for something else altogether.

"I was sick, just sick, about giving her money," Isabella stammered while still managing to sip her wine with grace. "I paid her in cash because I didn't want to have to see her name on one of my checks. Besides, I figured she understood being paid that way."

I couldn't help but laugh, and Isabella joined in. "At least you're free," I said. "I was so worried about you."

She smiled at me and reached her arm over to momentarily touch my leg. We were sitting on the front porch again, drinking away another night without any men at our sides. "I'm sorry I didn't tell you about what happened sooner, Charlotte. I was so depressed. I stayed in bed for days."

"What about work? Did you call in sick?" I asked, worried that her preoccupation with the whore and her inability to collect on the life insurance policy might eventually leave her with money problems on top of everything else. I didn't want to lose my neighbor due to a defaulted mortgage. But I also asked out of curiosity, curiosity as to whether she really had any job to worry about.

"Oh, Charlotte," she sighed. "I've lost my husband. I lost my house to a fire. Worst of all, I'm on probation for killing a phone that deserved to die a long time ago." Her voice trailed. "I don't care about work."

"You didn't call in at all?"

She sipped at her wine again, looked out into the trees, and laughed. But she didn't answer me.

The time passed slowly, and our words were few. I knew I had to ask her, and I almost did several times. I opened my mouth more than once with the words on my lips ready to be spoken, but it was as if I was afraid to know, afraid that she would be brutally honest, as she sometimes was, rather than vague and ambiguous, as she also could be.

When I finally managed to say the words, they came out fast. "How did the fire start?"

Isabella had finished her wine, but the glass was still in her hand. She didn't look at me for a long time. I knew she heard my question because her face changed. Her features, particularly her eyes, lowered, and there was a sadness in her expression that I had never seen before.

"I don't know," she whispered.

Again I hesitated. *She must know something. She must have asked questions. She must know the fire chief's conclusions.* Before I could gather the courage to ask, she offered me more.

"They say the fire started in the family room near the couch. They keep talking about burn marks or a pattern. Something like that." She paused again, but her eyes did not move. She was looking into the darkness with such intensity that I never saw her blink. "They found him on the floor ... He was probably trying to get out, but the smoke got him ... He didn't actually die from the fire so much as the smoke."

I bit down on my lip. "Why do they think you did it?"

She smiled faintly and shrugged. "Because I had a motive. Simple as that."

I remembered what Robert had told me and asked, "Had you been fighting?"

"Anthony and I always fought. That was nothing new."

I hesitated again, not certain how far to push the matter, but I couldn't help myself. "Where were you when it happened?"

She sighed slowly but did not look at me. "So Robbie has talked to you then," she said. "I wondered when he would say something."

"Why do you think that?"

"Because his firm has been fighting with my lawyer over the insurance proceeds, and he obviously knows that my inability to account for my whereabouts is my greatest weakness." Her voice was soft and steady. She looked at me now. "But you knew that, right?"

I was ashamed and embarrassed. "He just told me. I didn't know before—"

"It's okay. I understand." She stood up and walked to the front of the porch. "We need to get away from here, Charlotte."

"What do you mean?"

"We need to get away from this porch," she whispered and then turned to me. "You need to get away from this house."

"Why?" I asked.

"Because this house is keeping you prisoner, Charlotte." Her voice was a whisper, her words slightly louder than a summer breeze. If I hadn't seen her mouth moving, I might not have been able to figure out what she was saying. "There's so much more than this. You deserve better."

"How did *I* get into this discussion?" I asked.

"Well, my goodness, Charlotte, I thought you put yourself into it."

"Isabella, I simply asked you—"

"Don't be like him, Charlotte," she said, her voice slightly louder now and accusatory. "Don't play games with me. If you want to know whether I did it or not, then just ask."

I stared at her. My stomach felt sour and hollow. "Did you?"

She smiled in her usual flirtatious way. "Do you really want to know the answer to that?"

My eyes began to sting. "Yes," I whispered.

There was a short silence, and then she laughed again. "Of course not, Charlotte. I was probably capable of killing him. That I won't deny. But I wouldn't have burned down my own house in the process. I loved that house."

Chapter 15

The very next morning, after unsuccessfully doing an Internet search for information on the death of Isabella's husband, I dropped Willie off at camp and then drove to the college library. It wasn't a large or very modern library, but at least it had the last five years of the local newspaper on microfiche. The woman at the front desk—her name was Linda—helped me set up and then left me to wander through the past six months of papers.

I didn't know the month of Anthony's death, but Isabella said it happened in early spring. To be thorough, I began to scroll through the daily newspapers beginning in February for news of a doctor's tragic and fiery death.

It wasn't long before I spotted the first article. He had died in March, and the event had made the front page of the local section. The headline read PROMINENT ONCOLOGIST DIES IN SUSPICIOUS FIRE. The story read as follows:

> Dr. Anthony Capello, 41, a prominent oncologist at Brickwell Memorial Hospital, was pronounced dead on Saturday after a fire engulfed his house in the neighboring town of Lewisville. An autopsy has been performed, but a full report is not expected for several weeks. Preliminary reports, however, indicate that Dr. Capello died of carbon monoxide poisoning and severe burns after his house caught fire around 7:00 p.m. Saturday night. At least one fire official, who requested anonymity, commented that the fire appeared suspicious based on the suspected site of origin and other circumstantial evidence that he would not yet elaborate on.

The Brickwell Fire Department has promised a full investigation of the matter. Because of the suspicious nature of the fire and the resulting death, the State Fire Marshall, through the Fire and Explosion Investigation Unit (FIU) of the State Police, will also be involved in the investigation.

Dr. Capello, who has treated cancer patients in the area for more than a decade, leaves behind a wife, Isabella. She was not available for comment when this article went to press.

Several days later, another article appeared. This article was on the third page of the front section and was headlined, FIRE THAT CAUSED DOCTOR'S TRAGIC DEATH RULED SUSPICIOUS. The article, which was accompanied by a picture of the young doctor, read,

The fire that took the life of Dr. Anthony Capello this past Saturday has been ruled suspicious by fire officials investigating the matter. The *Brickwell Times* has learned from confidential sources that an accelerant may have been used to set the fire in the family room of the Capellos' home and that it may have taken only minutes for flashover to occur, making it almost impossible for Dr. Capello to escape. The State Police would not comment but did confirm that its Fire Investigation Unit (FIU) is still investigating the matter in conjunction with the Brickwell Fire Department.

Isabella Capello, the doctor's widow, has remained in seclusion since Saturday, but she released a statement through her lawyer early Monday to deny any involvement in the fire.

"At this point in the investigation, we are not prepared to rule this an arson case. Once we receive the autopsy results and complete an analysis of the [fire's] point of origin, we will be in a much better position to evaluate the matter," State Police Chief Ronald Hanson said. "We expect to complete the investigation and secure the autopsy results within the next few weeks."

The next significant article on the case appeared over three weeks later. The heading caught my attention immediately. DOCTOR'S WIFE QUESTIONED ABOUT DEADLY FIRE. As I read, my heart raced.

Isabella Capello, the widow of Dr. Anthony Capello, who died in a suspicious fire, was questioned yesterday by the State Police after an independent fire investigator hired by the Koswell Insurance Company, the carrier on Dr. Capello's life insurance policy, determined that the fire was a result of arson. Mrs. Capello continues to proclaim her innocence and neither the Fire Investigation Unit (FIU) of the State Police Department nor the Brickwell Fire Department has made any official determination of arson, claiming instead that they are still investigating the matter.

James Kastor, a fire investigator who is certified by the International Association of Arson Investigators or IAAI, determined that the fire was started near the couch in the first floor family room and that gasoline was used as an accelerant. His arson determination was based primarily on the presence of gasoline in floor samples taken from the area of the couch and the speed with which fire engulfed the rear of the house before being extinguished.

Mr. Kastor's report, a copy of which was obtained by the *Brickwell Times*, also makes reference to burn patterns as indicative of arson. The report notes, for example, that a large area of carpet and related padding in the center of the family room had been burned away, leaving an irregular burn pattern on the floor. The bottom of the door leading from the family room into the adjacent kitchen was also charred, which Investigator Kastor identifies as an indication that a liquid accelerant was used.

I closed my eyes and rubbed the corners with my fingers. I could hear my own heartbeat in the silence of the library. It pounded with such force that I was sure the thumps were visible through my cotton blouse.

If Isabella had killed her husband, how would it affect how I viewed her? Would I still be her friend? Or would I force her out of my life? It was not an easy question for me. Perhaps that's what haunted me the most—the possibility that I might be able to accept her alleged crime simply because I liked her, simply because she brought me comfort in a period of extreme loneliness. I read on.

The Kastor report, which is still being reviewed by police and fire investigators, also notes that several windows in the family room were open, which was not unusual given that Brickwell County is in the midst of a warm spring. Rather than provide an opportunity for escape, these open windows served to fuel the fire with air and to further increase the speed with which it spread up and out of the house. The Kastor report theorizes that Dr. Capello was asleep on the couch when the fire started and that he was too overcome by carbon monoxide poisoning to escape when he finally awoke.

I kept turning the knob of the microfiche machine, anxiously searching for more news of Isabella, her husband, and the mysterious fire. It didn't take long before I found another article. This time the heading read, WIFE IS IDENTIFIED AS ONLY SUSPECT IN ARSON DEATH OF HUSBAND. My heart sank as my eyes eagerly scanned the words that followed.

For a second time, State Police questioned Isabella Capello, age 35, in connection with the death of her husband, Dr. Anthony Capello, in a fire back in March. The questioning of Mrs. Capello, which lasted nearly five hours, came on the heels of a determination by the State Police, in conjunction with the Brickwell Fire Department, that the fire was a result of arson and was likely started by gasoline while Dr. Capello, a prominent oncologist, slept on the couch.

An independent insurance investigator, James Kastor, who was hired by Dr. Capello's life insurance carrier, had earlier determined that the fire was caused by arson. The Fire Investigation Unit of the State Police and local fire officials have now officially adopted the conclusions of Kastor's report.

An autopsy report confirms that Dr. Capello died from carbon monoxide poisoning and that he also suffered from severe, but nonlethal, burns. The autopsy report, a copy of which was recently obtained by the *Brickwell Times*, also revealed that Dr. Capello had been drinking the night of the fire and had a blood alcohol content of 0.18, which is far above the legal driving limit. The doctor's intoxicated condition may explain why he didn't immediately wake when the fire started.

"We were able to confirm that this is indeed an arson case based on lab results which indicate that gasoline was poured on the floor in the area of the couch. There also appears to be a pour pattern from the couch to the kitchen area," State Police Chief Ronald Hanson stated at a news conference last evening. "Mrs. Capello was with her husband shortly before the fire, as confirmed by witnesses who overheard her and her husband fighting less than an hour before the fire erupted. Mrs. Capello is unable to confirm her whereabouts thereafter but has indicated that she went for a drive to cool off and that the fire had already started by the time she returned home."

Chief Hanson added, "We have not yet made an arrest in this case, but an arrest is expected in the near future."

I stopped reading and leaned back in my chair. My head swam with questions, with confusion. I closed my eyes and tried to catch my breath.

"Is everything all right?" he asked. Startled, I jerked forward. Before I could answer, he said, "Sorry. I didn't mean to frighten you."

It was Michael Spain. He was standing next to the microfiche machine, a curious expression on his face. "I was just deep in thought," I said, a bit nervous. "What are you doing here?"

"I work here. Remember?" He was still very businesslike, but he had softened a bit from when we had spoken that first time. "And you?"

I fidgeted, uncomfortable sitting beneath his curious gaze. "I'm just doing some research," I said, pointing at the screen. I was amazed that he had even bothered to stop and talk to me.

"What are you researching?" he asked, leaning forward slightly. "From the look on your face, it must be something a bit unnerving." He spoke in smooth, even tones as he directed his eyes to the screen of the machine. I saw his lips move slightly as he began to read the article. His expression immediately soured. He looked at me curiously. "Why are you reading about Dr. Capello?"

I tilted my head and squinted, the glare of the overhead fluorescents suddenly bothering my eyes. "Did you know him?" I asked.

Michael had an odd look on his face, an expression that seemed to reflect a mixture of anger and sorrow. He didn't immediately answer, and the pause in his reaction quickly became uncomfortable. Just when I was about to speak again, he said, "Yes, I knew him. He lectured at the school occasionally. How do you know him?"

"I don't really," I said, not sure how to explain myself. He continued to look at me curiously, and I stuttered an explanation. "I know his wife. I was curious how he died."

Michael's voice was flat. "How do you know his wife?"

In our previous two meetings, Michael Spain had barely bothered to look at me, never mind say more than a few words. But now he was different. Now he seemed anxious, and for the life of me, I couldn't figure out why. Did he know Isabella?

"She lives next door," I said cautiously, fearful even as I spoke that I was saying too much. Why was he so interested in the doctor or his wife?

"Next door?" he asked, his voice rising slightly.

"Yes, on the other side of me."

There was a brief pause. He appeared stunned.

"Do you know her?" I asked. There were only a few people in the library, one or two in the stacks and a few others sitting alone at one of the tables toward the middle of the building. It was very quiet, almost too quiet.

"No," he said. "I don't know her. I'm just surprised she's our neighbor. I had no idea."

It seemed a perfectly logical explanation, but there was more to his reaction than he was letting on. Of that I was certain. "Did you know Dr. Capello very well?" I asked.

He nodded his head several times before answering "Yes, pretty well." There was a pause again, then he continued, "Most of the professors knew him." He appeared to want to say more, but he stopped himself. "Wasn't his wife charged with killing him?" he asked. "Aren't they claiming that she started the fire?"

I felt embarrassment heat up my cheeks. "I don't think she's ever been arrested, but I really don't know much about it," I said.

"Well, you must know enough that it piqued your interest. Otherwise you wouldn't be in here on a beautiful summer day looking at old newspaper articles." He kept his eyes on me.

"My husband's a lawyer. His firm is involved . . . for the life insurance carrier. Isabella and I have become friends. I really don't think she had anything to do with it, but I was curious what the papers had reported."

I was rambling, stumbling for an explanation, feeling completely stupid that I had gotten caught prying into my neighbor's history.

"I see," he said. "So you think she's innocent, and you want to prove that to your husband." His words were gentle enough, without any noticeable hint of judgment.

"You might say that," I agreed, relieved that he had explained my interest in Dr. Capello better than I had been able. Of course, there was much more to my mission than proving Robert wrong, but I had no need to discuss such things with Michael Spain.

"Well, good luck," he said, smiling slightly. He nodded as if to say good-bye, and began to walk away. I followed him with my eyes and saw him stop, his back still toward me. He hesitated briefly before he turned around and said, "Let me know what you find out. Just seems like I should know whether a neighbor of ours is a felon."

He didn't wait for a response but simply turned back around, his head lowered in thought. I watched silently as he walked toward the doors of the library and exited.

Chapter 16

*B*efore leaving the library, I read through a few more articles. Several articles were critical of the police for not immediately issuing a warrant for Isabella's arrest following the arson determination. These articles, which quoted several angry friends and family members of Isabella's husband, also contained speculation by several anonymous sources that an arrest warrant was being delayed due to undisclosed disagreements between the office of the state fire marshal and the local fire department.

One recent article also reported that Isabella's attorney had retained a fire investigator with a PhD in chemistry to do an independent evaluation of the fire's origin and cause. Apparently, Isabella's investigator was reinterviewing witnesses to the fire, speaking with state and local officials regarding their investigation and evaluating the evidence already gathered. There was also an indication that he had accessed the house, which remained standing in its burned and unsecured condition, to collect additional samples of the wood flooring and whatever carpet and padding remained. Although he had refused a formal interview, he was quoted to complain about the destruction of evidence, namely the furniture that had been located in the family room, the suspected point of origin.

After reading every last article I could find, I thanked Linda at the reference desk for her help, grabbed my things, and headed outside. It was still warm and sunny when I exited the library. As I walked to my car, the heat burning at my cheeks, I wondered why Isabella had not told me more about her husband's death or the likelihood of her imminent arrest. She had not even mentioned that her lawyer had hired an investigator to assist in her anticipated defense.

It seemed odd that she had not said more to me despite the many conversations we shared. Most of our talks occurred over a bottle of red wine, which I would have expected to loosen her lips. Then again, it certainly wasn't an easy topic for her, regardless of her guilt or innocence, particularly since the fire and her husband's death had occurred less than six months ago.

And why was Michael Spain so affected by my interest in Dr. Capello? Had he known him better than he was letting on? Had he known Isabella? I doubted that. Wouldn't he have recognized her at some point during his brief sojourns from the house on Wooster Street? Then again, Isabella rarely showed her face during the day and never turned her lights on at night.

It occurred to me that I could ask Jannie about Dr. Capello. I made a mental note to pursue that with her the next time we met.

When I arrived home less than twenty minutes later, there was a police cruiser in Isabella's driveway. The lights weren't flashing, and the siren wasn't on. In fact, I didn't see anyone outside the house as I drove past and pulled into my driveway.

I immediately got out of my car and walked up to Isabella's back fence. I had no qualms about peering over now, and I did so. I couldn't see much, however, and was forced to retreat back into the house for a better look from the vantage of my precious windows.

It was not usually difficult to spy into Isabella's house as she had no need for privacy and never closed her blinds. I ran from window to window on my first floor, trying to gain a glimpse of someone inside her house. I could see many things—her furniture, some laundry she had stacked on her couch, even a few empty glasses on her kitchen table—but I could not see her or any police officer. The house appeared empty.

I ran upstairs. Maybe she was on the second floor, perhaps gathering some clothes or personal items in anticipation of her arrest (did one need such things for prison?). When I reached the top of the stairs, I immediately went to the window in the upstairs hall to look over at Isabella's second floor. That's when I knew something was amiss.

Isabella's bedroom was in the front of her house. There were two windows on my side. Until today, however, I never even knew there were blinds on those windows. But I saw them now. I saw them because they were closed for the first time since I had moved in.

"Son of a gun," I whispered, both angered and concerned. "What the hell is she up to now?"

I stood at the hall window for several minutes, waiting for her to open the blinds or to show herself. She didn't, and I finally decided to call her. I went into my bedroom, my heart pounding, and dialed her number. I didn't call Isabella often. She hated the phone and usually didn't answer it, even when she was home. I had told her on numerous occasions to get caller ID so she could simply screen the whore's calls and retrieve the rest, but she always shrugged it off. "Why do I need to see who's calling?" she would say. "If someone has something important to say, they can visit me in person and tell me to my face."

"If you're not going to answer your phone, then why bother having one?" I had asked her once.

Her response was quick and simple, "I have a phone for making calls, not for receiving them."

As I expected, Isabella did not pick up the phone. Nor could I leave a message, because she still did not have an answering machine. Frustrated, I resolved to simply go over there and find out what was going on.

I went out the front door and walked down the porch steps. As I walked over to Isabella's, I tried to craft what I would say and decided to keep it simple. I would ask her if everything was all right. I was her neighbor and friend after all. It made perfect sense for me to inquire into such things, especially with a police cruiser parked in her driveway.

I rang the doorbell and waited. At least a minute passed before I rang it again. As I waited for a response, I cautiously tried to look into the front windows, but Isabella had closed the curtains there as well as if she had expected someone to appear on her steps for a closer look. What the heck was going on?

When Isabella still didn't answer the doorbell after the second ring, I started to knock. That's when I heard the car door shut and the engine start. I walked over to the driveway side of her front porch and watched as the cruiser drove in reverse toward where I stood. The officer sitting inside, whom I immediately recognized, did not wave or stop. He simply pulled out of the driveway and sped away.

I leaned forward over the front porch rail and look down the side of Isabella's house. She was standing in the driveway, just outside the back gate to her yard, her hands folded beneath her chest. She was smiling at me with that familiar glint in her eyes.

"What's going on?" I yelled.

She shook her head as if amused by my nosiness, and then began to laugh. Without saying a word, she held up her hand and signaled for me to wait a minute. Before long, she was inside the house, opening the front door.

"Aren't you supposed to be getting Willie from camp?" she asked cheerily as if nothing had happened.

"Normally, that's where I would be," I said suspiciously. "But he went to a friend's house after camp today and won't be home until after dinner."

"Oh," she sighed breathily. "Would you like some tea?"

"Why was Officer Lucarelli here?" I asked.

"How do you know his name?" she asked, her eyes widening.

"He introduced himself when he and his partner came looking for you a few weeks ago. Remember, the night you killed the whore's phone and went on the run for several hours?"

She laughed again. "Oh, yes. He was here that night, wasn't he?"

"Are you going to tell me what's going on?" I asked, still standing on the porch.

Isabella walked out and joined me. She was barefoot and wearing a low-cut sundress. "The police just like to keep tabs on me," she said.

"In your bedroom?" I asked, without forethought.

"I see you noticed the blinds," she whispered, raising her brows. "You don't miss a thing, do you, Charlotte?"

"It's not that I was being nosy," I said. "I got worried when I saw the police car. I thought you might have been arrested."

Isabella laughed. "Well, that should happen any day now, I suppose." She looked up at the sun, took a cleansing breath, and closed her eyes. A short time passed before she spoke again. "Officer Lucarelli is trying to help me, that's all. He believes I'm innocent, and he's trying to help me prove it."

"By sleeping with you?" I asked. I wasn't so direct with anyone but Isabella. It was the only way to get anything out of her.

Isabella did not laugh or flip her hair as I would have expected. She didn't even smile for that matter. Instead, she looked at me seriously, a slight glint in her eyes. "He's a good man, Charlotte. There's not too many of those left anymore."

"But Isabella—" I started.

"Don't worry so much, Charlotte. Things will work themselves out. They always do."

It was one of the few times that Isabella's self-confidence did not comfort me. I was worried for her despite the horror of what she might have done. Isabella may have killed her husband, but she was keeping me alive. Without her, I would have been alone, alone and desperate for a reason to struggle through each day. Our conversations, her simple presence gave me something to look forward to when the world seemed dark and empty. As I stood on Isabella's front porch that day, I couldn't imagine living on Wooster Street without her. It was then, in fact, that I realized why I needed to save Isabella from what she had probably done. I needed to save her because it was the only way I knew how to save myself.

Chapter 17

*I*sabella and I spoke for several more minutes before I walked back home. She never did confirm her affair with the police officer, but I understood the situation clear enough. Isabella was a beautiful single woman at a difficult time in her life. Officer Lucarelli, whatever his true beliefs as to her guilt or innocence, had plenty of reason to want to comfort her, even if it meant risking his livelihood.

Isabella was that kind of person. She made you want to do things you might never have done had you not met her, things you might otherwise deny yourself capable of. She was like alcohol. She impaired your judgment and made you see the world differently, making it easy to rationalize behavior that you would have easily criticized others for. She was excitement and temptation against a backdrop of mystery. Although these are the things that make men lust, they are also the things that awaken those of us, like myself, who are so depressed and bored with their lives that the presence of someone so strong and spirited becomes like water—a necessary element of daily existence.

As I walked up my front porch steps, I caught his figure in the corner of my eye. He was partially hidden in the shade of his own porch, but he stepped into the sunlight when I looked over.

"Is everything all right over there?" he asked.

"Next door?" I answered, still distracted by my own thoughts and startled by his voice.

"Yes. I saw the cruiser."

I nodded. "Everything's fine." It was unlike me to be short in my words, but I didn't have much to say. For once, I was not anxious for conversation.

He eyed me suspiciously, his hands dug deep in his back trouser pockets.

"I'm not used to seeing you out at this time of day," I offered, still standing on my own front porch.

"I decided to finally use my grill. I haven't used it yet this summer." His voice trailed off, and his eyes wandered. "Where's Willie? I haven't seen him around."

"He's at a friend's house. He's staying there for dinner."

"Your husband working late again?"

I smiled a little at his question, remembering back to when he had watched me through the windows. As distant and unfriendly as he could be, Michael Spain was a lot like me. He was lonely. And apparently he paid attention, at least when he was home. How else would he have known of my husband's habitual lateness?

"Yes, seems he's become a workaholic," I answered. "It'll be quiet though without Willie in the house."

He nodded as if he understood. "Well . . . ," he stammered. "Enjoy your night." With his hands still in his back pockets, he started toward his front door. I watched him open the screen and pause, just like he had at the library that morning. Without turning around, he asked, "I'm cooking some burgers if you want one."

I didn't answer immediately, unsure at first if he was talking to me or someone inside his house. After all, he wasn't looking at me and his words were spoken in a hesitant manner.

"Excuse me?" I said.

Still holding the screen door in his right hand, he turned his head slightly, his eyes downcast. "I can cook you a burger if you like. I have extra."

I was flabbergasted. Michael Spain had avoided me for weeks, yet in a single day he had initiated two conversations and was now doling out a dinner invitation. "Sure," I answered. "Do you want me to bring something?"

"Nope. No need," he said, glancing up at me quickly. He nodded slightly and said, "I'll be in the backyard."

I shrugged, still dumbfounded by his offer. Momentarily forgetting about Isabella, I went inside to freshen up.

Chapter 18

When I walked into the Spains' backyard, I was oddly at ease. The sun was shining, and the air was warm. An occasional slight breeze brought some relief. Michael was at the grill with his back to me as I approached.

"Hello," I said, carrying a bottle of wine in my hand.

He turned and gestured with his hand. "Come on in."

I flipped the latch on the back gate and walked onto a stone pathway. It led to a small patio in front of his back porch. Placing the bottle of wine on the wrought iron table, I grabbed a free chair. "It's a beautiful night, isn't it?"

"Not bad," he said. "How would you like your burger?"

"Medium is fine," I said.

"Shouldn't be more than a few more minutes." He continued to grill, his back muscles moving slowly beneath his shirt each time he flipped one of the burgers. "Cheese?"

"Sure," I said. "Thanks for the invitation. I hadn't given much thought to dinner."

"This is about all I cook in the summer," he offered flatly. When he spoke, it was as if he was reading out loud but without any of the lilt or emotion I used when I read to Willie at night. If Michael Spain was filled with emotion, which is what I suspected, none of it surfaced on his face or in his words.

"My husband hasn't cooked or grilled anything all summer, so you're doing pretty good." I instantly felt guilty for complaining about Robert and grabbed the wine bottle. "Would you like a glass of wine?" I asked, looking around and realizing that I forgot the corkscrew.

Michael flipped two burgers onto the plate, covered them with a pot lid, and lowered the burner on the grill. "Let me grab a few glasses," he said, still avoiding my eyes as he walked past me and up the steps into the house.

My eyes followed him. He had a strong figure and a youthful gate. From behind, his pain was invisible, but his face told a different story. I was certain he was at least in his late forties, had maybe even reached fifty. I couldn't be sure of his age. Sorrow has a way of aging people beyond their true years.

"Here you go," he said, handing me a long-stemmed wineglass. He opened the bottle with a hand screw and poured for both of us. "I'm usually a beer drinker, but wine might be a nice change."

Michael returned to the grill and threw some food in a grill basket. Then he sat in a chair across the patio, keeping a safe distance. We both sipped from our glasses and searched for conversation.

"The burgers are done, but I hope you can wait a few minutes until we eat. I wanted to slow grill some vegetables."

"That's fine. It's a nice night. No need to rush." I sipped more wine and mentally reminded myself to maintain a slow pace. It took a long time to earn an invitation into the Spains' backyard. I didn't want to blow it by getting too tipsy.

Michael took a few more sips of his wine and then stood to turn the vegetables. He stood by the grill for an awkward length of time, finishing our meal and making our plates in silence. The sun was still high in the sky, but the clouds were beginning to thicken.

Michael brought a plate to me and set the condiments on the small wrought iron table. "Sorry, I don't have a table for us to sit at."

"No problem. It's nice just sitting here on the patio."

For the first time, Michael actually looked at me and smiled. "You're pretty amenable," he said. "I can see where Willie gets his easy disposition."

"I'll take that as a compliment." I smiled back. "Willie's a great kid." Squirting a little ketchup on the bun, I dug a little deeper. "Do you have any kids?" I knew the answer, of course. Jannie had already told me about their two sons, but I wasn't supposed to know that, and it seemed like a logical question I would have otherwise asked.

"I have two sons," he said. "One's in graduate school in Boston. The other recently took a job in San Francisco."

"Do you get to see them much?" I asked, slowly nibbling at my food.

Michael shrugged. "I see my younger son Paul every few weeks, but Michael hasn't been home since . . . well, I'm hoping he'll fly back before the summer ends."

I knew he was thinking of her. The pain was evident in his voice. Did his sons blame him for the breakup? Is that why his older son moved away? "It must be tough to have your children grow up and live their own lives. I can't imagine what I would do without Willie."

We all had our pains to bear. Mine was living with Robert, and Michael's was living without Jannie or his kids. "How about their mother? Was that tough on her?"

Michael bit into his burger and chewed hard. Trying not to appear too knowledgeable or apparent in my eagerness for a response, I stabbed at the vegetables on my plate and took a large bite. The two of us sat on the patio for too many uncomfortable seconds, the sun still beating at our faces through the thickening clouds, before Michael answered, "My wife loved having the boys around. It was a little hard on her when they went to college and moved out. But she was always good at keeping them close by. You know, by doing their laundry, making a great Sunday dinner."

My glass was empty, and Michael stood to pour me a refill. The wine was easing the tension for both of us.

"Where is your wife?" I asked quickly before fear could seize my tongue into silence.

"What do you mean?" He took an absent sip of his wine.

My heart raced a little. "You seem to live alone."

"So do you," he said. When he saw the pain register in my face, he winced. "I'm sorry. That came out wrong."

"It's okay." I shrugged. "I *am* alone a lot. Robert took on this new job and has been working a lot of late nights to prove himself. He's a lawyer, you know. Just made partner. It's a very competitive environment for him now. He's still trying to prove himself." My words seemed genuine, at least so I thought, but inside I felt ill. Even my miserable neighbor saw what was going on at my house, probably pitied me more than I pitied him, yet here I was making excuses for Robert, defending him while he slowly planned his escape from my life.

I swallowed a long stream of wine, instantly feeling the warmth travel to my stomach. Michael stood up and began to clean the grill. "I'm sorry," he said. "Sometimes I should just keep my mouth shut." He scrubbed the brush against the metal slats, scraping away flakes of burned meat and grease. "My wife always told me that I was a bad communicator."

"Is that why you're not together anymore?" I asked, covering my plate with my napkin. I was no longer hungry.

Michael stopped scrubbing and turned around, the brush still in his right hand. "Is that what you think? That I'm divorced?"

"Well, you're not wearing a ring," I said, surprising myself by such quick thinking. I wasn't usually very good on my feet.

"Aren't we the little investigator," he said, a smirk now forming on his lips. "Did you research my life at the library as well?"

"So that's what you think of me. That I'm a nosy neighbor?"

There seemed to be a glint in his eyes. Maybe it was just the effect of a falling sun. Maybe it was the wine. He too was on a second glass. "Maybe just a little. You were conducting research on Dr. Capello after all. Not your everyday research project."

"I think you're avoiding the subject," I said, but it wasn't the right thing to say. The glint quickly left his eyes, and his face looked heavy again.

"I don't really like to talk about my wife," he said.

"I'm sorry. I didn't mean to pry." I waited a moment, but he said nothing. "See, you're not the only one with bad communication skills."

Michael sighed. "It's a nice night. We still have an hour or so of light, and the wine tastes good. Why don't we just stay away from the subject of our personal lives and stick to happier subjects?"

"It's a deal," I said, somewhat relieved. "Only Willie should be coming home soon, so . . ."

"Do you think he'll be hungry?" Michael asked. "I can throw another burger on the grill if you think he'll want one."

"I already ate dinner!" Willie yelled, running up to the gate. I stood and waved at Mrs. Simpson across the yard and watched as she began backing out of my driveway. Willie walked through the gate and threw his backpack on the grass. "But I'm not too stuffed for desert!"

Chapter 19

Michael, Willie, and I sat in the backyard, talking and laughing for the next hour. Willie entertained us with his impressions of superheroes and his descriptions of the monsters he had invented in summer camp. He was animated and excited to be in Michael's company. I couldn't help but wonder why he didn't have such an easygoing and joyful relationship with his own father.

Willie was one of those kids who made everyone feel welcome and comfortable. He had been that way even as a baby, always smiling and cooing, even when complete strangers leaned over with their oversized heads and ogling eyes to get a better look at the sweet baby. Yet it still surprised me to see how effortlessly he pulled Michael from earthly withdrawal and made him whole again, transforming him from a bystander into a willing and eager participant in conversation and laughter.

When the sun fully set and the yards had darkened to a dull shade of black, I helped Michael carry the condiments and plates back into the kitchen. It was the first time I had ever entered his house, and I was not at all surprised to find it neat and tidy and simple. We all said good night, and after much resistance and attempted bribery, Willie headed off to bed, a handful of comic books in his hands that Michael had pulled from a shelf in his son's room. "Take good care of those," he had politely warned Willie. "My Michael will notice any bent corners or wrinkled pages."

Despite the late hour, Robert was not yet home. After folding some laundry and cleaning up the first floor, I returned to the back porch to take a final look at the stars. As usual, there were no lights on in Isabella's house. She had probably met Officer Lucarelli somewhere more private, where my probing eyes wouldn't catch them in the act again. I sighed. I hadn't thought about Isabella all night, but now the worries came racing back. What was she doing fooling around with that officer? Did she think it would help her get off the arson charges?

"Deep in thought?" he said through the darkness.

I jumped, startled by the sound of his voice. It took me a moment to register his face in the darkness of the backyard. "You scared me," I said, pulling my hand to my chest.

"I'm sorry. I didn't mean to. I saw you sitting there and thought you might like to share one last glass of wine before we called it a night." Michael had the bottle in his hand and two empty glasses.

"Maybe one last glass," I said. "Then I have to stop or risk waking up with a headache."

"Tomorrow's Saturday. Can't you sleep in a little?" he asked, sitting down next to me. He poured us each a glass and placed the bottle on the porch between our chairs.

"You obviously don't remember how early little six-year-old boys wake up in the morning."

"Oh yeah. I forgot about that."

"It's getting a little chilly. I think I'll grab a sweater," I said. "Do you need anything?"

"No. I'm fine, thanks."

When I returned from the house, Michael was standing against the railing, looking out over the lawn. "I'm sorry about what I said earlier," he said. "About you living alone." He turned around to face me. "You know what they say. Misery loves company."

"Are you miserable?" I asked, leaning back in the chair.

"Not all the time. Sometimes I guess." He sighed and looked at me curiously. "Are you?"

I thought about his question, but I didn't have to. I knew the answer instantly. I just didn't know if I wanted to say it out loud.

"There I go again. The whole 'bad communicator' thing."

"You're not that bad. You must have been good enough to hold a conversation with Jannie for your marriage to last so long."

Michael grimaced and lowered his glass. "How do you know her name?"

I stammered, realizing I had screwed up. "You said it earlier, during dinner."

Michael looked at me and shook his head. "No, I didn't. I almost never say her name anymore. Not to strangers."

"I didn't realize I was still a stranger," I said, a little hurt.

"Did you talk to some of the neighbors? Did someone say something to you about her?" He looked over at Isabella's house. "Did Dr. Capello's wife say something?"

"Why would Isabella say something about your wife?" I asked.

Michael looked at me a while longer, puzzlement in his face. "You can keep the bottle," he said. "I'm going to call it a night."

"Michael, wait," I said, standing up. "I'm sorry. I'm not trying to be evasive. It's just that she told me not to say anything, and I didn't want to cause a problem."

"Mrs. Capello? Why would she tell you not to say anything?"

"Not Isabella," I said, confused. "Jannie. I talked to her a few times when you weren't home. She asked me not to mention it."

"What are you talking about?" he said, a hint of anger now in his voice.

"She was sitting in the backyard and I said hello—"

"That's impossible," he charged.

"No, it's the truth. She came by when you weren't home. She didn't want me to say anything. She thought you might get upset that we talked about your . . . situation."

He looked at me with such an odd look that I didn't know how to react or what to say. He stared at me for a few long seconds before marching down the porch steps and flinging his wineglass against the back fence.

"What is it with you people and pitching things into the yard?" I yelled, running after him. He struggled to open the gate and then turned back to me.

"I thought you were a nice woman, Charlotte. I thought that maybe we could help each other. But for you to say such things. I don't understand it."

"What are you talking about? I only talked to her a few times. Why are you getting so angry?"

"My wife is dead, Charlotte. She doesn't sit on back porches, and she doesn't talk to the neighbors anymore."

"What? No, she's not."

He shook his head, looking both irate and bewildered. "She's been dead for eight months, Charlotte." Then something registered with him. I could see it in the changed expression on his face. "Did your friend Mrs. Capello tell you about Jannie? Did she tell you the whole ugly story?"

"Michael, I'm confused. Why would Isabella know anything about your wife?"

"I'm not a fool, Charlotte."

"I never said you were."

"I'm not going to buy into some lame story about how you can talk to ghosts. I've had it up to my fucking eyeballs with all of the psychics and mediums who claim they can talk to my wife and then end up saying a bunch of ambiguous crap that would never have come out of her mouth. Jannie was many things, many wonderful things, but she was not ambiguous."

Michael marched into his yard, slamming the gate behind him. I couldn't speak. I couldn't even breathe. What was he saying? And why the hell was he pulling Isabella into all this?

Jannie *was* alive. I had seen her clear as day, had spoken to her several times, had seen her on the couch and at the dinner table. Willie had seen her too, in the backyard and on the roof. The roof . . . Dear God, the roof.

Chapter 20

"*I* swear, Isabella, you better answer the goddamn door," I yelled, pounding on the old wood. It was almost ten o'clock, but I didn't care. She had known something about Michael Spain all along and had never said a damn thing about it. She was going to come clean with me if I had to stand at her door and pound until morning.

I didn't stay there all night, but I stayed longer than I should have, pounding like a lunatic, stabbing at her doorbell every few seconds. Soon my hand ached and my anger released long enough for the realization to sink in that Isabella simply was not home. Because she didn't answer the phone or have an answering machine, I couldn't even vent my emotions by calling her. It was all starting to make sense—why Isabella didn't answer her phone, why she didn't have caller ID, why she didn't have an answering machine. She was avoiding stress, stress from the people she filled with it.

As I was walking home, Robert pulled into the driveway. I was so furious from the night's events that I stood there and stared at him in judgment for the first time in our marriage. He stumbled out of the car. It was clear he had been drinking. When he approached me, I could smell the perfume on his clothes. Oddly, I didn't feel jealousy or sadness or pity for myself. It was worse than that. I felt hatred—pure, angry hatred—an emotion so deep and vile that my stomach felt as if it was rotting away right then and there in the driveway.

When he passed by me and didn't so much as apologize or offer an excuse, even a lame one, but instead chose to judge me with those eyes of his, I did something I had never done or contemplated before. I kicked him in the ass so hard that he fell flat on his face into the pavement, scraping a large chunk of skin off his forehead. His briefcase and car keys flew out of his hands and skipped down the drive as his body smashed against the blacktop. Without stopping to help him up or survey his injuries, I picked up his keys, walked into the house through the back door and locked him out.

It's odd how things have a way of coming around. First, Isabella pitched her phone in the yard. Then Michael pitched his glass. First I pounded on Isabella's door in fury, and now Robert was pounding on ours. I couldn't let him in. Now that I was inside and had calmed down, the realization of what I had done began to sink in. Robert was drunk and bleeding and very angry. He had never hit me before. He never had to. I was the obedient, forgiving wife who never asked a difficult question simply because I never wanted a truthful answer. My life was as phony as the superheroes and monsters of Willie's imagination.

But now, now I didn't know what Robert would do. He was angrier than I had ever seen him, more physical and verbal than I had ever witnessed. I thought about calling the cops but hesitated. Did I want to be the neighbor everyone talked about, the one with the drunken, cheating husband? If I called the cops, I would suddenly become the poor, pitiful wife, the one who was emotionally beaten into submission, the one fearful for her life, the one too stupid to walk away and too homely to keep her husband interested in her. It was bad enough to be a victim, even worse to be one in the public's eyes.

I had to do something. If the noise continued, Willie would certainly wake up. I grabbed the phone and dialed Isabella's number. Why did I bother? Of course she wouldn't pick up. Why did I still look to her for help after all the lies and deceit? I hung up and thought about calling Michael. Even if he was mad at me, I believed he would still come to my aid. The only problem was that I didn't know his phone number. I started to dial the police. I had no choice. I had to do it for Willie's sake.

Before I could finish dialing, the knocking stopped. I pushed the button on the phone and hung it back on the receiver. Had he left? Had he passed out? Leaving the phone on the table in the family room, where I had hid in the shadows during the ruckus, I started for the kitchen cautiously. Had he gotten into the house? Shit! Did he know about the key beneath the flowerpot, the one I had left for Willie in case of emergencies?

I peeked into the kitchen, but the door was closed. I would have heard that squeaky hinge if he had gotten in, wouldn't I? I scanned the room and edged toward the window. The lights were still on in the kitchen, which made it difficult to see outside. As I neared the back windows, I finally saw him. He was lying on the porch, his face flat on the ground. Standing behind him, a large rotary phone in her hand, was Isabella, a look of guilty pleasure on her face.

"My god," I shouted. "Did you kill him?"

"You're not that lucky, Charlotte," she said, dropping the phone with a loud clang. "I only hit him with the receiver, not the whole goddamn thing. You're lucky I saved this little antique. Who knew phones could be so useful?"

I was at a loss for words. As usual, Isabella filled me with mixed emotions as she stood there in her perfect clothes and makeup, not an errant piece of hair or a missing accoutrement to complain of. I didn't know whether to thank her or to strangle her. "What do I do now? What if he's hurt?"

"He's so drunk, Charlotte. He probably won't remember any of this. What's a little brain damage to a lawyer anyway?" She laughed at her own joke.

"Isabella!" I screamed and started to cry.

"Oh for heaven's sake," she said, bending over to grab his arms. "If it were me, I'd leave him out here. But for your sake, I'll help you drag the bastard inside." She grabbed him from under his arms and showed amazing strength in turning his body around so that he was face up. "Prop open the door and then grab hold of his legs," she directed. I did as she told me. He was incredibly heavy for a thin guy with only five feet ten inches to his frame.

We carried him in through the kitchen and, after almost dropping him twice, finally managed to maneuver him onto the couch. "His head looks awfully bloody," I said. "But he seems to be breathing okay."

"Head wounds always bleed a lot. I wouldn't worry about it, except he's probably going to mess up your couch." Isabella was wearing a tight-fitted dress and had on three-inch heels, which only made her physical abilities even more curious.

"How the hell did you carry him in those heels?" I asked.

"Expensive shoes provide good balance," she said without a second thought.

We both stood in silence for a few minutes, occasionally glimpsing at Robert to study his horrible wound and to make sure he was still breathing normally. At least that's what I was looking at. Isabella simply seemed amused.

"Where did you come from anyway?" I asked. "I pounded on your door earlier and then I called, but you didn't pick up. Did you just get home?"

"No, Charlotte. I heard you. I even saw you kick that bastard in the ass. I couldn't stop laughing. I would still be laughing if he wasn't making such a ruckus on your door."

"You let me stand there and bang on your door while you pretended to be gone. How could you do that? What if I needed you? What kind of friend does that?"

Isabella lifted one brow and eyed me indignantly. "I didn't open the door for the same reason you didn't open the door for Robert. You were mad as hell, Charlotte. It would have been a waste of time talking to you while you were in that condition. Besides, I didn't feel like being judged."

"Being judged? Do you even know why I came over?" Robert was still unconscious on the couch, but we both momentarily forgot his presence.

"I assume to scold me for sleeping with Officer Lucarelli. It's not what you think, Charlotte." Isabella stood with her hands on her hips, one high-heeled foot placed delicately in front of the other. She had poise even in awkward and angry moments, and it was really starting to irritate me.

"No, actually. I came to talk to you about—"

"What the hell is going on over here?" Michael said after barging through the kitchen door and rushing through the archway into the family room. He was half dressed, wearing only a pair of blue jeans, and his hair was wet. Even in such uncomfortable circumstances, I couldn't help but look at his bare chest with some fascination.

Isabella turned. When she saw Michael standing there, she flinched noticeably. Her eyes met his with an intensity I had not seen before. She appeared stunned and confused, perhaps even a little fearful.

Michael looked at her bewildered. He too seemed ill at ease. "I live next door. I just got out of the shower and saw you two carrying someone through the door." Michael then noticed Robert on the couch, blood splattered across his face from the wound on his forehead. "Jesus, what the hell happened to him?"

"He was born with testicles and then grew up to be a lawyer," Isabella quipped, her eyes finally dropping from his direction.

"That's not funny," I said, turning to Michael. "This is Isabella. Based on your accusations earlier, I presume you already know her."

Isabella stretched out her perfectly manicured hand. "Actually, I don't think we've met," she said, still a bit apprehensive. "You must be Michael Spain, the other neighbor."

Michael shook her hand, his expression difficult to read. "Isabella Capello?" he asked, but it was more like a statement than a question. "Dr. Capello's wife."

Isabella let go of his hand. Then she turned to me. "What did Mr. Spain accuse you of, Charlotte? And why do you think we know each other?"

Robert began to murmur and struggled to sit up. "I better get some ice for his head," I said, rushing into the kitchen.

"Charlotte," Michael called after me, trailing me into the kitchen. "What happened to him? Don't you think we should call a doctor?"

I grabbed a gallon-sized ziplock bag and filled it with ice. "He fell in the driveway," I said. "It's just a scrape on his forehead." I started back into the family room where Robert was now sitting, his head in his hands.

"It looks like more than a scrape," Michael said.

"Head wounds bleed a lot. They look worse than they really are," Isabella offered for the second time. "Charlotte, maybe you should stay with me tonight."

"I can't leave Willie," I said, holding the ice to Robert's forehead. He hadn't spoken yet and still seemed groggy.

"Is someone going to tell me what happened here?" Michael pressed.

"I already told you, Michael. I think we can handle it from here." I was still angry at him for his earlier accusations, not to mention a little concerned about his odd claims of having a dead wife.

"Who the hell slammed my head into the driveway?" Robert asked, his voice unsteady. Michael eyed me and Isabella.

"You fell, Robert," I said. "You had too much to drink."

As his consciousness came back, Robert's voice got louder and meaner. "No, I didn't. I was pushed! Then someone hit me on the head when I was on the porch. I'm not an idiot, Charlotte!"

"That's debatable," Isabella whispered.

Robert stood suddenly. "You fucking pushed me into the pavement," he yelled, turning toward me, his face twisted with fury. "And then you smashed something into my fucking head." He grabbed hold of both my arms and started to shake me. "Who the hell do you think you are!"

Michael grabbed hold of Robert from behind, wrapping his bare arms around Robert's and pulling him backward. Robert's grip let loose, and I took a step away from him, my body shaking uncontrollably. Glaring at me with loathing in his eyes, Robert struggled to break free from Michael's hold, but Michael had him in a firm grip and was not letting go.

"You need to calm down and back off!" he warned Robert.

Robert struggled for a few seconds more before easing the tension in his arms. "Just let me go," he said, his wrath still apparent. "I'm not going to touch her."

Michael kept hold, while Robert's eyes seized mine. They burned with such abhorrence that I felt small and weak again in my own home. It was then that I realized how much Robert truly despised me. The sad thing is, I had no idea why.

"Let's go upstairs and check on Willie," Isabella said. She walked past Michael and Robert, still linked by the arms, and gently guided me to the stairway. Turning back as we walked, she said, "Make sure he leaves this house tonight . . . without a key."

Isabella and I went upstairs and checked on Willie. It wasn't until I entered my own bedroom that I let the sobs flow. Isabella showed her friendship that night and sat with me for hours. For the first time since we had met all those weeks ago, she had nothing sarcastic or mysterious to say.

Chapter 21

*I*sabella and I both fell asleep on the bed, fully clothed and exhausted from the events of the night. At about 3:00 a.m., I awoke in a sweat and scrambled to my feet. I changed into more comfortable clothes and worked my way downstairs. I had no idea where Robert had gone, but I had seen him leave in a cab, with Michael watching from the end of the driveway. As angry as Michael had been with me, he made sure Isabella and I were safe. Or maybe his concern lay with Willie. Whatever the situation, he had been there for us, and I would be forever thankful.

I walked into the kitchen and poured myself a glass of ice water. It was either the wine I had with Michael or all the crying that had left my body dehydrated and thirsty. I didn't actually see him until I started back through the family room. There he was, sleeping on the couch, an old blanket wrapped around his body. Michael Spain had come back inside to watch over us.

I stood there for a moment, stunned by the complexities of the man sleeping soundly on my couch. He had been angry enough to scream at me in my own backyard yet caring enough to come to my rescue when I needed it most. He had been both selfish and selfless in the span of one mysterious night.

I adjusted the blanket to provide him with more cover and started back to my bedroom. Something made me turn back and look out the window toward Michael's house. Unlike most nights, there was no flicker of light from the television set and no one sitting on the couch in silence. Instead, something more intriguing captured my attention. Jannie was there. She was standing at the window looking at me, a faint, understanding smile on her face.

Chapter 22

*D*espite the early hour, Isabella had already gone when I woke up the second time that morning. I was anxious to get downstairs before Willie, before he saw the neighbor sleeping in our family room and started asking questions I couldn't answer. I quickly found Willie sitting on the couch watching cartoons by himself.

"Hi, buddy," I said, looking into the kitchen. It appeared empty.

"Hi, Mom."

"Did you already eat breakfast?"

"No. I just came down." He sat there on the couch in his Superman pajamas, his hair ruffled on his head, his feet crossed Indian-style. He was so happy and peaceful. I longed to be in the same place, but I knew that innocent state of being had left my life long ago.

I sat down next to him and held him tight, kissing his cheek and then his forehead. "Mom, you're squeezing me!"

"Because I love you," I whispered in his ear and kissed him again.

"I know," he sighed, his eyes still fixated on the television.

"Want some cereal?" I asked, standing.

He looked up and smiled. "Can I eat in here? *Please?*"

I cupped his beautiful face in my hands and weakened. "Maybe this one time."

"Yeah!" he cheered. "Thanks, Mom."

"Sure thing."

I walked into the kitchen, my mind now drifting back to the horrible events of the night. Would Robert come home? Would he cause another scene? Where was he? Had he gone to her house? Who was she anyway? Another lawyer, a judge, a secretary?

I poured Willie's cereal and set it on the coffee table in the family room, careful to put down a place mat to absorb the inevitable spills and overflows. I never let Willie eat outside the kitchen, but today was different. Today I wasn't in the mood for enforcing rules.

I made a pot of coffee and sat at the kitchen table. Even with Willie happily watching cartoons in the next room, scooping so much milk and cereal onto his spoon that I could hear him munching loudly, it was perhaps the loneliest I had felt in a long time. It wasn't so much that Robert wasn't home. He was almost never home anymore anyway. No, it was more than that. It was the realization that I had become so tolerant of him that I had lost myself. I had allowed him to despise me, to treat me poorly in front of my own son. I had allowed him to have no accountability, no reason for regret or remorse. I had made it so easy for him to be distant and so uncaring that he finally showed his cheating ways without a passing thought or apology. Isabella was right. I had been a whore in my own home, letting him pay the bills while I waited for him to want me.

What would I do now? What would I do if Robert walked back through the door today or tomorrow or the next day and things went back to the way they had been for the last year or two? How long *had* it been this bad? It had started long before the move and had only gotten worse since. The pain and self-loathing bubbled in my stomach like hot acid. I felt ill and scared and sorry for myself. The tears started to come, and I couldn't stop them. I pulled the tablecloth up to my mouth and stifled the sobs. I couldn't let Willie hear my pain. I couldn't let him see my weakness.

When I had drained as much emotion as would come so early in the morning, I stepped outside for some fresh air. I took a deep breath in a desperate attempt to cleanse myself. It was sunny and warm, just as it had been almost every day that summer. I could smell the flowers in the back, the lilacs especially, and it brought me some momentary joy.

The peacefulness was short-lived. The moment I saw Isabella walking out of Michael's house, my heart felt heavy and tired again as if every beat was closer to being the last. Isabella saw me as soon as she started down the back porch, and she paused for a moment before continuing to step down onto the stone patio. I couldn't take my eyes off her. It was the first time she appeared disheveled and soiled. Her hair had not been brushed, and her eye makeup had started to crawl down her face. Even her dress, the same one she had on the night before, didn't seem to fit. It was frumpy and wrinkled. Isabella looked tired and worn and completely unhappy.

"Have you heard from him?" she asked, and it took me a moment to realize she was talking about Robert.

"No," I answered in a half whisper. "What were you doing over there?" I nodded toward Michael's house and then scanned the windows to see if he was watching. I couldn't see anything in the glare of the sunshine.

"Nothing important," she said, but her voice was flat. She didn't even try to put on a show. This was a side to Isabella I had never seen before.

"Talking about your pathetic neighbor maybe," I accused, a hint of anger in my voice. But I had no right to be angry. They had both come to my assistance when I needed it most. So why then did it bother me so much to see Isabella coming out of Michael's house?

Isabella didn't stop her pace. She opened the gate and walked into my yard without any further hesitation. When she reached the bottom of the stairs leading up to my porch, she looked up at me with sad eyes. "Do you think I can have some of that coffee?" she asked.

Chapter 23

"You're not going to let him back, are you?" Isabella asked half accusingly. She had been drinking her coffee in silence up until now, looking somewhat defeated and sorrowful.

"I don't know," I said. It was the truth. I didn't want Robert back, at least not the man he was now. I wanted the old Robert, the one I had fallen in love with, the one I still loved. But he didn't exist anymore, and I felt myself mourning his loss. How would I survive on my own? I had long ago learned to live without affection or romance, but I was still financially dependent on Robert.

"Why would you ever want him back?" Isabella asked. She was direct but not her dramatic self. "He's only going to bring you more misery, Charlotte."

"How did you survive when you lost your husband?" I asked. "How do you manage?"

Isabella shrugged. "I'm a survivor. I had no choice."

"But how do you manage financially? You don't seem to have a job ... they've been fighting you on your insurance money. How do you even pay for the house you're living in?"

Isabella sipped at her coffee and looked out the kitchen window into the backyard. "I told you, I work at the salon. That's how I survive."

"Do you really think I'm that stupid, Isabella? I know you don't work at a salon or cut hair. Where do you really go when you're not home?"

Isabella looked at me and then rubbed both of her eyes. One of her red-painted nails was chipped. The flaws were starting to show themselves. Isabella was falling apart, just like me.

"I'm going to be arrested soon," she said. "John held them off as long as he could, but everyone is convinced of my guilt and want to bring this thing to an end."

"John?" I asked.

"Officer Lucarelli," she said. "Do you mind?" she asked, lifting her empty coffee mug and rising to her feet.

"No, go ahead. There's plenty. I'm just going to check on Willie."

As Isabella poured herself another cup of coffee, I went into the family room. Willie was lying down on the couch, still mesmerized by the television set. The cereal bowl was empty, but there was a spattering of cereal and dried milk on the place mat. I picked up the remnants of breakfast and said, "Another half hour, and then I want you to get dressed. It's too nice outside for you to be hanging in here watching TV."

"Michael said he'd take me to the batting cages today if it was all right with you."

"You spoke to Mr. Spain this morning?"

"He was standing on the back porch when I woke up. You were still sleeping." Willie's eyes didn't leave the television set. "So can I go with him?"

"What was he doing on the back porch?" I asked.

"I dunno," he said, shrugging. "I think he was bringing us the paper. I put it on the table."

"Let me think about the batting cages," I said. "Mr. Spain was probably just being nice. I'm sure he has a lot to do today."

"No, he doesn't. He told me so." Willie was looking at me now, that pleading look in his face. "Please, Mom?"

"We'll see," I said and walked back into the kitchen. Isabella was sitting down again, with her chin resting lazily on her hand. I put the dirty dishes in the sink, refilled my coffee mug, and stood by the open back door. The screen allowed the warm air in. It felt good against my skin.

Isabella didn't speak for several minutes. When she did, she changed my world. "You're right, Charlotte. I haven't been working at the salon. I used to, ages ago. I can probably still give a pretty good haircut." She sipped at her coffee, her eyes fixated on the backyard.

"So what have you been doing, Isabella?" I asked. I took a seat at the table across from her. I could hear the murmur of the television and Willie's occasional giggle.

"Sometimes I go to church," she said. There was still no sparkle, no glimmer of hope or happiness in her expression. "It's true. I do. I have even gone to confession. Other times I go to the cemetery and stare at his grave, maybe even curse at him a little for being so cruel, for turning me into someone I wasn't meant to be."

The sun was rising higher, and the heat penetrated through the window with such intensity that I stood to partially close the curtains. Isabella didn't seem to register my movement and kept talking.

"Sometimes I go to the whore's house. I have even followed her around town a few times just to see what she's doing and who she's whoring around with." Isabella turned the coffee mug in her hands and watched the creamy fluid swirl around inside. "Mostly she's at the hospital all day, where Anthony used to spend all of his time. She's a goddamn nurse, so sweet and patient and kind to the cancer patients. If they only knew what she was really like. If they only knew she was a husband-stealing bitch with bad phone etiquette."

Isabella threw her head back and laughed at herself. She shook her head in disbelief, letting me know how amazed she was at where she had ended up in life. Then, for the first time since our conversation began, she looked me in the eyes. A tear skipped down her cheek and dropped heavily on the tablecloth. It was the same tablecloth I had cried into less than an hour ago. "I was a good wife, Charlotte. I was always there for him when he came home at night. I didn't stray even though I had plenty of opportunity. All those surgeons at the dinner parties and holidays. I could have had any one of them, could have pulled them into a closet and done whatever I pleased. They wouldn't have given two thoughts about their wives. But I didn't. I honored my marriage for a long time . . . as long as I could."

"What do you mean?" I asked.

"I got lonely, Charlotte, and I got angry. I started hanging out at night when he didn't come home. That's how I met John. He was nice to me. He gave me everything Anthony didn't."

"So you knew Officer Lucarelli before the fire?" I asked, surprised by this development but uncertain what it meant.

"Yes, I knew him for months before the fire. Anthony was working such long hours, dealing with cancer patients all day long. For every patient he saved, there were so many more he lost. He couldn't handle it. He started drinking. He started cheating on me. He started doing whatever he wanted, whenever he wanted. In his mind, he had earned the right to be reckless and free. He was trying to save lives every day. He thought he was entitled to a little fun after what he was forced to witness and fight. The fading lives, the crumbling families, the loss of hope, the loss of life."

Isabella closed her eyes and then rested her forehead in her hands. "He started out as a good man, a good doctor. He ended up a bastard and a drunk. And I ended up miserable, miserable and angry. So angry that I had to look outside my marriage for a little happiness."

I wondered if that was why Michael had reacted the way he did at the library. Perhaps he knew that Dr. Capello had a drinking problem. Perhaps he knew he was a womanizer. Then I remembered the night before and Michael's angry rant. "Did your husband know Janice Spain, Michael's wife?"

Isabella lifted her head. "Janice Spain?" she said, tilting her head slightly. "I don't know. Was she a patient of his?"

"I don't know. Michael said something about it last night, about you knowing her."

Isabella sighed. "Anthony had so many patients. He talked about some of them, but he didn't usually use their names. I think it was easier for him to think about them in a more abstract way. He would say 'this patient' or 'that patient,' but I almost never heard their names."

Isabella tried another sip of her coffee, but it had turned cold, and she quickly lowered her mug. "But if she was a patient of his, that wouldn't have been a good thing."

"Why?" I asked.

"Anthony was an oncologist. He only treated cancer patients ... Many of them didn't make it." She paused, staring into her coffee mug. "Didn't you say you met her recently?"

"Yes," I said, more to myself than to her. I thought back to last night. I thought of Jannie standing in Michael's house, smiling at me in the darkness. It was so odd, almost as if I was dreaming, but she was there. It wasn't possible she was dead.

Isabella eyed me suspiciously as if she wanted to say more. Apparently thinking better of it, she simply said, "I'm tired, Charlotte. I think I need to go home."

"We need to finish this, Isabella. You need to tell me what happened that night."

"You have enough on your plate, Charlotte. Worry about solving your own problems. Mine may be beyond repair." She stood up, leaving her coffee mug on the table.

"Please," I said. "Maybe I can help you."

Isabella smiled and pulled me close for a hug. "You are a good person, Charlotte. You deserve better than you got." She let go and grabbed hold of my shoulders. "Learn from my mistakes, sweetheart. If you hold on for too long, you may do something you will never forgive yourself for."

Chapter 24

*I*sabella was gone for half an hour before my doorbell rang. It startled me. Willie was upstairs changing, and I had just taken a shower. I threw on my robe and looked down the stairwell to see who was at the front door. It was Michael Spain.

"I was hoping you would let me take Willie to the batting cages today. Did he talk to you about that?" he asked, his face expressionless as if nothing unusual had passed between us.

"I spoke to Willie, but I'm not sure it's a good idea," I said. "But I do want to thank you for last night . . . for helping me."

"Has he come back?" he asked, his words still flat.

"No."

Michael frowned. "I know you're angry with me," he said, "about last night, about what I said to you in the backyard. What you said upset me. I didn't understand. I don't understand."

"Neither do I," I replied. "I saw someone at your house, Michael, someone who said she was Jannie. I had no reason to think otherwise. I didn't just make that up as part of some scam."

"I know that now. My head's a little clearer." He scratched at his forehead and sighed. "But it wasn't my wife. I don't know who you saw, but Jannie passed away eight months ago." He pulled his wallet from his back pocket and retrieved a laminated card, lifting it toward me. It was the size of a business card, and I saw at once that it was an obituary.

"It probably seems odd that I laminated it, but I keep it on me, mostly because it's a good picture of her. I look at it sometimes when I'm having a bad day." His eyes drifted.

I pulled my robe tighter and looked at the picture of the woman on the card. It was indeed Jannie, the same woman I had seen at Michael's house, the same woman Willie had seen. My throat tightened. It became difficult to fill my lungs with air.

"Are you all right?" Michael asked, but I barely heard him.

I stared at the woman in black and white. She was pretty and a bit younger than the woman I had seen, the woman I had spoken to several times. I tried to convince myself that it was someone else, that the person in the photograph was somehow different than the woman I had met, the woman who called herself Jannie and said she had left her husband. *Left her husband?*

"Charlotte, what's the matter?" Michael asked, but I couldn't look at him. Had he made this up? Had he forged this obituary? How could this be?

"I don't understand," I said. My brain felt cloudy, heavy.

"What don't you understand?" he asked. "Is that who you saw?"

The muscles in my legs started to quiver and the laminated card blurred before my eyes. The air seemed so thick and damp, hard to process. "I can't breathe." I felt myself falling sideways, felt my weight shift to the left. Michael grabbed me and helped me back inside. He sat me down in a chair in the front room.

"What's the matter?" he asked. "Was it the picture, Charlotte?"

"I didn't eat any breakfast," I said. My ears were plugged, and the words coming from my own mouth sounded odd, as if I was talking underwater. I leaned back against the chair and tried to take a deep breath.

Michael stood, leaving the laminated card in my grasp. "I'll go get you some juice. That might help." He started for the kitchen, but I grabbed his hand.

"Don't say anything to Willie," I said, squeezing his palm. His hand was so foreign to my touch that I felt an odd sensation when he squeezed back, his grip firm and strong.

"Okay," he said, a hint of worry still on his face. "I'll be right back." He walked into my kitchen. I heard him open the refrigerator and search the cabinets for a glass. It was a small old house, and noise traveled easily from one room to the next.

I stared at Jannie's photograph. How could this be? Did she have a twin? Had she faked her own death? Was Michael Spain simply making this all up?

"Mom," Willie yelled as he jumped down the stairs in his shorts and T-shirt. "Is Michael here? I thought I heard him. Is he here?"

I hid the picture in my hand. "He's in the kitchen getting me some juice."

Willie gave me a questioning look.

"He's being nice. I was thirsty."

He stared at me for a moment and, without a word, gave me a quick hug and kiss on the cheek. "I'll go help him," he said, smiling again, and ran into the kitchen. The fact that he had not yet asked me about Robert was telling.

I was mesmerized by her photograph. It was indeed the woman who claimed to have "left" her husband after twenty-seven years of marriage, the one who said they were not divorced, the one who didn't want me to tell Michael I had seen her, the one who played on the roof. If she wasn't real, if she hadn't been in the backyard or in the family room watching television late at night, and if she hadn't been on the roof, then why had I seen her? Why had Willie seen her? I believed in God and heaven and everything else I learned in church, but I didn't believe in ghosts. That was the stuff of movies and books and late night television.

Michael came back quickly with the juice and kneeled down in front of me. He handed me the glass without a word and searched my face for answers. I took a small sip and then handed back his laminated card. He looked at it briefly before returning it to his wallet.

"Is that the woman you saw in my yard?" he asked. It was the most emotion I had ever heard in his voice. I could not tell what answer he was hoping for.

"I don't know," I lied. "I'm not myself yet. Maybe I should lie down."

There was a flicker of disappointment in his face. "Does it look like her, like the person you saw?" he persisted.

"There's a resemblance," I offered, "I just don't know." I closed my eyes. My head was still spinning. Michael remained kneeling where he was, curiously silent. I couldn't open my eyes and look at him again. I didn't have the nerve to see his pain or confront the big question that floated in the air between us—had I really seen Jannie?

Michael placed a soft, reassuring pat on my knee and then finally stood. "Let me take Willie to the cages," he said. "It will give you a chance to get some rest."

I opened my eyes now, only to see Willie behind Michael in mock prayer, pleading with frantic lips and dramatic expressions of hope and excitement.

I was hesitant under the circumstances. I didn't know what to make of the situation with Jannie. I didn't know what to make of Michael Spain. But he had taken care of me, and he had shown true kindness toward Willie. Besides, there was something I needed to do, and I didn't want Willie with me when I did it.

"Okay, but how long will you be gone?" I asked.

"Two hours tops," he said. "I'll take him to the cages, and then maybe we'll grab some lunch. Does that sound good, Willie?"

"Absolutely!" Willie was overjoyed. He ran to put on his sneakers. He had learned to tie them by himself months ago.

"Where are the cages?" I asked.

"I'll take him to the Lakewood batting cages. They're only about ten or fifteen minutes from here." Michael bent forward slightly and looked at me with worried eyes. "Get some rest," he said. "We can talk later." Then, standing fully upright again, he looked back toward Willie. "Come on, champ. Time's a-wastin'."

"Wait," I said, sitting up. "Do you have a cell phone? In case I need to reach you?"

Michael pulled his wallet from his back pocket, the same wallet that held the laminated obituary. He pulled out his business card. "All of my information is on there," he said, "including my cell phone number."

"Okay, thanks," I said.

Willie quickly tied his sneakers and was out the front door before I had even left the chair. After they had driven off and the house was quiet again, I made my way upstairs, still a bit unstable on my feet, and put on a pair of shorts and a T-shirt. After grabbing some toast to ease my stomach, I sat at my computer and searched for *Pinewood Cemetery*, the funeral location identified in the laminated obituary. If Jannie had truly died, as Michael had claimed, there would be a headstone to attest to her passage. Obituaries could be forged, but headstones were another matter. As I wrote down the directions to the cemetery, it suddenly dawned on me. If no headstone existed for Janice Spain at Pinewood Cemetery, then the obituary was almost certainly a fake, and I had just made the biggest mistake of my life by letting Michael take my son.

Chapter 25

I had not been in a cemetery since my father had passed two years ago from an unexpected heart attack. It had been quite a blow to my family. My mother was still struggling with his loss, but she managed. She had a strong circle of family and friends to help her cope.

I parked the car on the side of the ring road and tried to figure out where to start my search. I had less than two hours before I needed to get home for Willie. Like most cemeteries, this one was quite large. It was not all that difficult, however, to figure out which sections had long been closed to burials and which ones held the newly deceased. The newer headstones were straight and clean and easy to read, unlike some of the older monuments whose chiseled words had chipped and faded with the passage of time and the onslaught of Mother Nature. Many of the older stones had tilted to one side as the ground below decayed and shifted with the seasons. I felt a sense of loss for the strangers who had been buried there.

Even the color of the grass was different in the older areas of the cemetery, a mixture of green and brown, reminiscent of wet fallen leaves that had languished on the ground for too long without nourishment. The grass in the new areas, however, was a brighter, more optimistic green, a color that still gave one hope that life did indeed go on, even in difficult times.

I drove around the ring road until I found a section of the cemetery with the newer headstones. I parked and got out of the car. There was a slight breeze, but the air was warm. I walked my way through the aisles of stone, careful to take note of the dates of death. I was in the right place.

There were children and grandparents, mothers and fathers. There were stones that told stories and others that told of the sadness left behind. Then there were the stones with no words at all except the person's name and their dates of birth and death. It was as if nothing of note had occurred during the time span between the beginning and ending of their life. There were no carved images on these sad stones. No chiseled words of remembrance. No plastic flowers in the vases to let the world know that someone had been there to visit and remember them. Were these souls as lost and lonely in heaven as they must have been on earth? Was that my own destiny, to die with nothing worth writing on my headstone?

I walked up and down each aisle, scanning the carved words for *Janice Spain* or *Jannie*. By the time I reached the end of the new section of stones, I was beginning to panic. She was not there. There was nothing to confirm that Michael's wife had been buried in this cemetery. My stomach dropped when I thought of Willie, my precious Willie. Was he all right?

After I had walked through the entire section of stones without any trace of Janice Spain, I ran back to the car and grabbed my cell phone from the center compartment. I dialed the cell number on Michael's card and listened while it rang. It rang four times before a message came on, a message with a robotic voice that told me the person I had called was unavailable. I could feel the panic rise from my belly and swim up to my throat. I took a deep breath and tried to remain calm, but there was no hiding the quiver in my voice.

"Hi, it's me, Charlotte. Just calling to make sure everything's okay. Call me back when you get this message. Thanks." I left my cell phone number and hung up. I didn't drive off immediately. I was angry at myself for not getting the directions to the batting cages before I left the house. Then again, if Michael and Willie were actually there and doing exactly what Michael had said they'd be doing, I'd have no reason for concern. So what was I supposed to do now? Wait and hope they returned?

I started driving around the ring road, my mind flooded with thoughts and worries, my heart racing with panic. I could lose Robert. I could lose my marriage. But I could never bear to lose Willie. He was my heart and soul. He was everything to me. Why would Michael lie about Jannie?

As I drove, a few droplets of rain hit against the windshield. I slowed and looked toward the sky. It was sunny and blue. There was but a single cloud, yet somehow it had managed to break open, and a sun shower hit unexpectedly. I put on the wipers and continued on. Despite the deep fear I now felt, I did not race around the road of the cemetery. It was too narrow and too near the outlying stones to accommodate fast driving.

As anxious as I was to escape this place and get back on the main road toward home, I could not risk knocking over a headstone in the process.

The rain continued to beat against my windshield. The wipers knocked rhythmically from side to side even as the sun shone bright through the glass. I had closed my windows, leaving the driver's side open just a crack, and I could smell the freshness in the air. Then I could smell the lilacs. Where were they? I could see the many oaks and pines and the smattering of plastic flowers near the headstones. There were even a few fresh flowers left at some of the graves. But I didn't see any lilac trees or bushes or anything else that might account for that smell, that beautiful, enticing smell that brought me back to my childhood.

I had grown up on a long, dead-end street. The road was not well traveled but still showed signs of heavy wear and tear and made my bicycle rumble when the tires hit all the loose stone that had broken away from the pavement over the years. On the opposite side of the street from where I had lived in a modest three-bedroom Cape Cod with my parents and my sister and brother, there was a small white house on a double lot with a long chain-link fence near the sidewalk. That fence was lined by an endless row of lilac bushes, whose purple blooms gave off such a flowery scent that I would always ride my bike along that side of the street just to get close to the enchanting smell.

Now, as I drove through Pinewood Cemetery, I smelled that same scent, and a flood of memories came rushing back into my mind. My life had been good when I was a child. I had been happy, unaware of the things I didn't have and totally appreciative of the few things I did. How had I ended up here? How had I ended up in a cemetery, searching for a woman who was clearly still alive and would have no reason for a headstone?

As I reached the last bend toward the road, the sun shower stopped, and I turned off the wiper blades. It was then that I noticed a clearing in the woods and saw that there was yet another section of headstones that appeared relatively new. One in particular was quite large. It was adorned with a tall white angel reaching toward the heavens, her broad wings arched back for flight, her body sheathed with a flowing dress that spoke of freedom and weightlessness. I pulled over and walked toward the image, the smell of lilacs still fresh in the air.

The grass was wet and a bit long. I could feel the dampness crawl through the sides of my sneakers as I neared the headstone, but there was nothing I could do. I had to get closer and see who had been so worthy of such a beautiful piece of sculpture. As I approached, the carved letters stood out clearly, even in the brightness of the summer sun. The name on the stone read "Janice Spain." My heart skipped, and I felt a searing but momentary pain in my chest. The rest of the inscription read, "Loving mother and wife, friend to all who knew her, beloved by many. She will be missed."

Jannie had died at the end of November, just eight months ago. There was nothing on the headstone to indicate how she had died, but I already knew. As I stood there, it became quite apparent to me why Michael had been so intrigued by my research at the library and by the revelation that Isabella Capello lived next door. Dr. Capello must have been Jannie's doctor. Poor Janice Spain, only forty-seven years old, must have succumbed to cancer.

It wasn't only Jannie's death that intrigued me. Her date of birth also struck me hard. She had been born on March 30, a date that was significant in my own life. Jannie was fifteen years older, but her birthday was the same as mine.

If Jannie was buried beneath the wet grass where I stood, then who was the woman who had spoken to me and my son, the woman who always smiled and who never had to yell to make her gentle words heard? Life on Wooster Street was strange indeed and getting stranger by the minute.

Chapter 26

When I pulled into the driveway, I instantly saw the police cruiser parked at Isabella's house. Officer Lucarelli was there arguing with the other officer who had visited me that late night a few weeks back, the one so badly in need of a manicure, the one who saw no humor in life and smoked too many cigarettes.

Isabella was already sitting in the backseat of the cruiser, her head lowered, showing the defeat I had seen in her earlier that day on the back porch. Officer Lucarelli was upset about something because he kept pointing his finger at Officer Johnson's chest and made no effort to lower his voice. When I exited my car, I could hear him arguing about the handcuffs. Poor Isabella must have been restrained before being placed in the patrol car.

I crossed Isabella's yard and headed toward the officers. As soon as they saw me, they stopped talking and faced forward.

"This is not your business, miss," Officer Johnson said, taking a few steps toward me.

"You have my best friend in the backseat of your car," I said. "What's going on?"

"Charlotte, you should go home," Officer Lucarelli cautioned. "I will take care of Isabella. There is nothing you can do for her."

I ignored them both and kept walking. "Isabella!" I yelled as I neared the car.

"Charlotte, go home. There's nothing you can do for her now." Officer Lucarelli grabbed my arm, and I quickly pulled myself free.

"You have no right to touch me," I said and then turned toward the car, where Isabella was stretching her neck forward to get a better look at the commotion. When she saw me, she smiled.

Officer Johnson stepped in front of me and put his hands up. "You better get away from the car, or we'll arrest you too for obstructing justice."

I thought about telling them that my husband was a lawyer and that they better not start trouble with me, even if my lawyer husband was sleeping around with someone at work, drove home drunk last night smelling of perfume, and hadn't called me in the last eighteen hours. I thought better of it and disregarded Robert altogether. "I just want to talk to her. I won't get in the car. Just let me say a few words through the window." When Officer Johnson simply stared at me with crossed arms and a look of indignation on his face, I added, "You can stand right next to me to make sure I don't do anything."

"It's all right, Tom. They're good friends," Officer Lucarelli said. "Just give her a minute."

Officer Johnson gave me a dirty look, even as he stepped to the side and let me pass. He followed me to the car and made me stand two feet away from the window. Isabella was inside, wearing a low-cut dress. Only Isabella could look that sexy with her hands cuffed behind her back, her cleavage all the more visible and accentuated from the uncomfortable position they had put her in.

"Are you okay?" I asked.

"I'm fine. I just want to get this over with," she said, and she seemed to mean it. She had been expecting her arrest as she had indicated this morning. It must have been horrible waiting for something so terrible and imminent.

"Do you want me to follow you? Did you call your lawyer?"

"They'll let me call him when I get to the station. Stay here, Charlotte. It'll be a boring, drawn-out process, and there's nothing you can do there. Hopefully, I'll get out on bail within a day or two."

"I'm sorry, Isabella," I said, my eyes welling up again with tears. I had cried more in the past twenty-four hours than I had all summer.

"Don't be sorry, Charlotte. Just be smart," she said. "You know what I mean, sweetie? And keep a bottle of wine in stock for me. I might need a few drinks after tonight."

With that, Officer Johnson ordered me away from the car. I walked backward half the distance across Isabella's front yard, unable to pull my eyes away. Officer Lucarelli gave me one last look, a look of reassurance maybe, before he slid into the passenger seat and drove off with his less sympathetic partner. I could see him shift in his seat toward Isabella, perhaps comforting her, as the cruiser pulled onto the street and drove away.

I stood in Isabella's yard even after the patrol car was out of sight. I was lost and alone and completely unsure what to do with myself. My best friend was being arrested for killing her husband, something she might very well have done. My other neighbor had a dead wife who managed to appear to me on several occasions to converse. And my husband had probably left me for another woman. It was depressing yet hysterical all at once.

I sat on the grass in Isabella's front yard and then let myself fall backward. Looking up into the smattering of clouds against the pale-blue sky, I let my mind go blank. I didn't want to think anymore. I just wanted to lie in the sun and let the world disappear. Only a few seconds passed, however, before thoughts of Willie jumped back into my head and made it impossible to lie still.

I looked at my watch. He should be home soon. Was there any reason to be concerned now? Michael had told me the truth. His wife had, in fact, died. She was buried exactly where the obituary had said she'd be buried. The thought that I may have spoken to a dead woman made my insides ache in a way I had never before experienced. Had she really been there? If Willie hadn't seen her too, I might have doubted myself. But he had seen her. We had both seen her. She was either the real Janice Spain or a look-alike fraud. Either scenario was frightening as hell.

Thankfully, Michael returned with Willie just as he had promised, with five minutes to spare. I had waited for them on the porch and saw how excited Willie was when he jumped out of Michael's car.

"Mom, you should've seen me. I hit almost every ball. It was awesome!" Willie ran up the steps and showed me his swing with the bat we had gotten him for his sixth birthday.

"He did very well," Michael said, placing one foot on the bottom step of the porch. "Are you feeling better?" he asked.

I nodded. "Yes, much better," I lied. "Thanks for taking him. Sounds like he had fun."

"Anytime."

"What do you say, Willie?"

"Thanks, Mr. Spain."

"Sure thing, Willie. I had a good time."

Willie opened the door and went back into the house, leaving me alone with Michael.

"He's a great kid. He should be signed up for Little League." Michael fidgeted with his keys as he spoke. He was different now, uncomfortable in my presence.

"I know. With the move and Robert's new job, it didn't work out this year. Maybe next season."

Michael nodded. "I think he'd like it." He twirled his keys around his finger and looked down at his own foot, which was nervously tapping at the bottom step. The arrogant confidence he once displayed to me was no longer there.

"You never really answered my question earlier," he said without looking up.

"What question was that?" I asked, but I knew exactly what he meant.

"Whether the woman you saw and spoke to was Jannie."

I was too tired to say anything but the truth. "The woman I met looks like your wife, like the woman in the picture you showed me. She said she was Jannie. She said she was your wife. I am as confused about this as you, Michael. I don't know what to think."

Michael stared at me with such intensity that I expected an onslaught of accusations and anger. Instead, he asked a question that caught me a little off guard. "What did she say to you?"

"She said that she left you last winter after twenty-seven years of marriage, that it was time to leave. I just assumed you had separated. I assumed you were getting a divorce."

He nodded and started to chew on the side of his mouth. The keys still jingled in his hand, and his foot played against the worn wooden step. "Where did you see her?" he asked.

"I saw her on the back porch. She was sitting in the rocker there."

This statement registered something with Michael, and he looked up, his eyes searching mine. He stopped jingling his keys. "Where was the rocker?"

"In the corner."

"In the shade or in the sun?"

"In the shade. Why?"

He closed his eyes and wiped roughly at his brow with his left hand. When he looked back up, he seemed troubled. "Anywhere else? Did you see her anywhere else?"

"Why are you asking me all of this?" I asked.

"I need to know. I need to know exactly what you saw."

"I don't even know if it was her, Michael. I don't see how it could be."

"Just tell me, Charlotte!" he demanded, startling me.

I stood up and started toward the door. "I think I should go in, Michael. Maybe we can talk about this later."

"Please!" he said. His voice was pleading, desperate. "Please tell me. I'm sorry. I didn't mean to raise my voice."

He stepped off the bottom step and shoved both of his hands into his back pockets. He looked small and defeated, just like Isabella had looked earlier. I hesitated, afraid of the strength of his remorse, but he looked so helpless standing there on my walkway, his defenses down. "I saw her several times at night, on the couch next to you, watching TV in the dark. And Willie saw her too."

"What? Willie saw her?" His eyes were misty now.

"Yes, Willie saw her twice." I didn't tell him about how Willie saw her on the roof the first time and how she tried to explain it away with a story about repairs. How could I possibly explain that?

Michael pulled his hands free and ran them roughly through his hair, scratching at his scalp. His head began to shake from side to side. "I don't understand."

"Michael, I don't understand either. I'm very confused by all of this, just as much as you are. But I wouldn't lie to you about something so important. Maybe it wasn't her. Does she have a sister or a cousin or someone in her family that looks like her?"

"No," he whispered. "I don't know. Maybe. She was adopted. Her sisters and brothers didn't really look like her." His voice was tinged with anxiety. He struggled to pull the wallet out of his back pocket, once again lifting the laminated obituary to show me her face, her pretty, caring face. "She looked like this, right?"

I nodded, staying where I was, close to the door just in case he lost control of his emotions. I turned and looked in. Willie wasn't in sight, which meant he had either gone upstairs or was in the kitchen. That was good.

"Did she say anything else?" I could see his mind struggling with the circumstances. I was doing a lot of struggling myself, but I didn't have any answers for him.

"Michael, all I know is that the woman I spoke to seemed very kind, very gentle. She expressed concern for you. She didn't even want me to tell you I had seen her. If it wasn't your wife—"

"Did she say anything about Dr. Capello?" he asked, his eyes searching my face, looking for answers beyond any words I could offer.

"No. Why? Was he her doctor? Did she die of cancer?"

Michael continued to rub at his face. He was quite anxious, quite agitated. "She didn't say anything at all about how she died?"

"No, Michael. I didn't know Jannie had died. The woman I saw was as real to me as you are now—"

"But she looked like the picture, right?" he asked, his voice uneven, the laminated card still held tight in his raised hand.

"Yes," I said softly, pity grabbing at my heart. I could see how painful this was, how he was now locking on to the possibility that his dead wife may have appeared to me. I wanted to run. I wanted to leave my front porch and retreat into the house. I wanted to stop thinking about Jannie. I wanted to find a rational explanation for all this, but it was eluding me.

"And you saw her in the rocking chair on the porch, in the corner in the shade?" His words came out fast but clear.

"Yes," I said.

He started nodding again. "And on the couch at night, next to me?"

"Yes."

"Okay. Thanks, Charlotte." He turned back toward his car, which he had parked in the street in front of my house. "Tell Willie I said good-bye." Michael then climbed into his car and started to drive. He didn't pull into his own driveway but kept on going. It would be days before I would see him again.

Chapter 27

Robert did not come home or call that night. I didn't see Isabella either. In the morning, when she still had not returned, I called the police station and inquired about her, but they wouldn't give me any information.

Willie had yet to ask about the whereabouts of his father. That alone was not so unusual as he had become accustomed to Robert's increasing absence. What struck me, however, was that he had instantly asked about Michael when he woke up and whether we could have him over for lunch.

"I think Michael took a short vacation," I said, peeking out the window into his empty house. I had peered out my windows throughout the night. I had even walked around the front of his house, but his car had never returned. No one had watched television in the darkness of the Spain living room either, and no one had returned to sit in the rocker on the porch. For these last few things, I was relieved. What would I do if I saw Jannie now?

"Why would he leave without saying good-bye?" Willie asked, his left brow slightly lifted.

"He did say good-bye. He told me to tell you." I ruffled my fingers through his scruffy hair. "He'll be back, Willie."

Willie pondered this for a moment and then asked, "What are we going to do today?"

"I dunno, kiddo. Looks like it's just you and me."

"I like you and me," he said, and his smile overwhelmed me. He was not his father, and for that I was so grateful.

I kissed him on the forehead and said, "Let's go out for breakfast, Willie. Then we can decide what to do the rest of the day."

"Okay," he agreed and walked to where his sneakers had been thrown to rest the night before.

Willie tied his shoes with careful deliberation, manipulating his tiny fingers to make each loop with precision. When he finished, he looked up with a sense of accomplishment and smiled his toothy smile.

Willie sat in the backseat as I drove to the local diner. "Willie," I asked, "do you remember when you saw Mrs. Spain on her roof?"

"Yeah."

"And when we spoke to her on the back porch?"

"Yeah, why?"

"Did she look different to you?"

"What do you mean?" he asked.

"Did she look funny to you?"

I looked in the rearview mirror and saw him scrunching his face. "Wadda ya mean, funny? Like silly?"

"No, not silly. Just different." I didn't know why I was asking him. I didn't really know what I was asking him. It just seemed to me that if it was Jannie we had spoken to, if Jannie had been a ghost, wouldn't she have looked different? Wouldn't she have seemed different? Maybe Willie had picked up on something I had missed.

Willie didn't say anything right away, and I kept driving. It was a beautiful, clear day, the kind of day that would usually bring me renewed hope and serenity. But my life was anything but serene at the moment, and I couldn't fully absorb the beauty around me. When I pulled into the parking lot of the diner about five minutes later, Willie finally spoke again and shook my world a little more.

"Was she a ghost, Mommy?"

I pulled into the closest parking space and turned to him. He showed no anxiety, no discomfort in the possibility of his words. "Do you think she was a ghost?" I asked.

"I thought she was a witch, but you and Daddy said she wasn't. So maybe she's just a ghost."

"Why do you think that?"

"Because she just disappeared off the roof," he said. Then, with a tilt of his head, he continued, "And she speaks weird."

"Weird?"

"Yeah." He paused and furrowed his brow. "She speaks in my head."

"In your head?"

"Yeah, not out loud like you. But in my head."

I was still sitting in the driver's seat, my body twisted toward him in the backseat. I released the seat belt and leaned against the steering wheel. I thought back to my conversations with Jannie. Her voice had indeed seemed soft and clear, even from a distance, like she had perfected the skill of projecting her voice without having to change her tone. But I had never made the observation that my six-year-old son had just made. Was he right? I thought back. Her lips had moved when she spoke, but had the sound come from her or from within me? I truly couldn't say.

"Mom?" Willie asked.

"Yes?" I whispered, my back still firm against the steering wheel.

"If she's a ghost, does that mean she's bad?"

"No, Willie. If she's a ghost, I think she's one of the nice ones."

"How do you know?"

I thought about this for a moment before I answered him, "Because a bad ghost is not just scary. A bad ghost makes you feel bad inside. And Jannie doesn't make me feel bad inside."

He pursed his lips and mulled this over for a few seconds. "I guess you're right. She scared me a little because I thought she was a witch. But she didn't make me feel bad, not like . . ." He stopped himself.

"Not like who?"

"Nothin'. Can we go inside? I'm hungry."

"Okay, buddy. Let's go."

Willie and I got out of the car, grabbed hands, and walked slowly up the steps of the diner. He never did tell me who he was talking about, but I knew. And it broke my heart.

Chapter 28

The next few days were the longest, most grueling days I had spent to date on Wooster Street. I had learned from Isabella's lawyer that she had been arraigned and her bail had been set, but she was stuck in jail, waiting for her family to wire the money from Italy. If I had the funds, I would have covered bail myself, but Robert had drained our accounts and still had not resurfaced. Willie finally had asked about his father, and I had made up a story about a business trip. But even a six-year-old can sense deceit.

As for Michael, he had stayed away. I searched his windows obsessively for signs of his return, but the house was dark and empty, like it had fallen ill and was riddled with despair over its own sickness. I felt pulled by that house, drawn to it, and my obsession seemed to worsen with each passing hour. I couldn't stop looking into the Spains' windows. I would stand at my own panes of glass and stare across the fence that separated our yards. I would look into that house and wonder, what was happening inside? Was Michael home? Had I missed his return?

More than anything else, though, I searched anxiously for signs of Jannie's presence—for a shadow, a flicker of light, a tug on the curtains. I strained to see if she was sitting on the back porch or on the family room couch. I imagined she was looking back at me, smiling, whispering her soft tones. I even kept close tabs on the roof, just in case she chose to return there. But there was nothing, nothing to indicate the presence of any life—or death, for that matter—in the Spains' house or on their roof. Finally, at the end of the third day since Michael's departure, I couldn't resist the urge any longer. I checked on Willie, who had fallen asleep hours earlier, and then walked out my back door and across the darkened yard.

The Spains' back door was locked as I suspected it would be. I walked silently up the drive on the opposite side of the house and checked the front door, but it was locked too. I checked the windows on the front porch, but they didn't budge. A certain level of insanity had crept into my soul, making it impossible to fight the need to access that house no matter what the cost. So I searched along the drive until I found a large enough stone to break the back-door window. Then, with that stone tight in my hand, I headed toward the yard.

"What are you doing, Charlotte?" she asked.

My breath caught. I stopped and strained to see through the shadows of the night.

"Why are you out here so late?"

The sound of my breath broke through the silence in the air. All I could see was her dark silhouette at the end of the driveway. The stone was cold in my hand, and I nearly dropped it when I realized who was speaking to me.

"Isabella?"

"Who else would be wearing high heels fresh out of the slammer?" she asked, with a slight shift of her curvy figure.

"Oh my god!" I instantly ran to her. She had been gone for only three days, but her absence had left me lonely and depressed, worried that she may never return, worried that I would be a lost soul without her. I pulled her close and kissed her cheek.

"My goodness, Charlotte," she whispered. "It's not like I've returned from the dead."

I pulled back but kept my hands on her arms. "But someone else may have," I whispered.

Isabella lifted one brow. "Please don't tell me Anthony came back."

"No, not him. Jannie. Janice Spain."

Isabella tilted her head. "Charlotte, what is your obsession with this woman?"

"Isabella, I have talked to her, actually seen her on numerous occasions, but Michael says she died, that she was a patient of your husband's."

Isabella said nothing, at least not with her painted lips. But her eyes spoke volumes.

"I'm not crazy, Isabella. I *have* seen her! I *have* spoken with her!"

"Charlotte," she said, now taking hold of my arms. Her grip was firm but tender. "I am really worried about you. Michael told me about his wife, how she died. It's simply impossible that you actually know her. She died long before you moved into this house."

"When did he tell you about his wife?"

The words lingered on her lips before she spoke them, "That morning. That morning after the incident with Robert." There was an apologetic look on her face when she continued, "I had gone next door to thank him for helping us, and he told me about his wife, about how Anthony was her doctor, about how she died. Remember? You saw me coming out of his house—"

"But I asked you about her that morning. You told me that you didn't know her. You pretended not to know if she was Anthony's patient."

"I didn't know anything about Michael's wife or her connection to Anthony until that morning. And when you asked about her, I didn't know what to say. I didn't know what was going on. Michael told me she had died months ago, but you claimed to be seeing her. It was all so confusing. So I lied. I'm sorry, Charlotte. I wasn't trying to hurt you."

"What else did he say to you that morning?" I asked.

"It doesn't matter, Charlotte."

"It does matter," I said.

"The point is that she is dead. I don't know how you know about her but—"

"She's not dead!" I argued. "Even Willie saw her!"

Isabella wrapped her arms around me. "Oh, Charlotte. This is what I've been warning you about, how men can make us so sad and lonely that we get a little crazy."

"I am not crazy," I said, pushing her away. I walked around her, into the backyard and up the Spains' back porch steps. I pulled open the screen door, which had not been locked, and then smashed one of the small windows of the rear door with the stone I had pulled from the side of the drive.

"Charlotte! What are you doing?" Isabella raced up the stairs after me, but I already had my hand through the broken glass and was twisting the lock open. Within seconds, I was entering the house.

"You're bleeding!" she cried.

I looked down at my hand and saw the cut. It wasn't deep, but there was a lot of blood on my wrist. "It's nothing."

"Charlotte, what the hell are you doing? You need to have that checked."

Isabella followed me inside. I stopped in the middle of the kitchen and turned to her. "You should leave, Isabella. You're out on bail. I can't imagine you want to be caught breaking and entering."

Isabella's eyes widened, and she slowly shook her head. "Have I done this to you, Charlotte? Have I made you think it's okay to be as crazy as me?"

She may have been right, but I ignored her question and walked toward the family room, the same room where I had seen Jannie, staring at me through the large window and sitting on the couch with her husband. I sat on that same couch and closed my eyes.

"Charlotte, are you okay?" Isabella asked as she followed me in. I felt her sit next to me. Then I felt her hand on my shoulder. "What can I do? How can I help?"

"You should leave," I said.

"I won't leave you, Charlotte. I'm worried about you." A few moments passed, and she spoke again. "What are we doing here?"

"I'm waiting for Jannie."

"She's not here, Charlotte," she whispered. "She's dead. She died many months ago."

"Tell me what you know," I said, but I kept where I was, my eyes still shut.

There was a long pause before Isabella answered me, "She was Anthony's patient." Her hand tightened on my shoulder. "Michael says he screwed up. That he caused her death."

"How?"

"Apparently, Jannie was referred to Anthony after she was diagnosed with breast cancer." Isabella shifted on the couch. "Anthony treated her very aggressively with chemotherapy."

I opened my eyes and turned toward her. "But it didn't work?"

"According to Michael, the chemo was too aggressive and not properly monitored. She developed a hole in her colon. Some kind of bacteria, I don't remember the name of it, got into her bloodstream." Isabella took a deep breath. "She died from her treatment, not the actual cancer itself."

"Michael blames your husband?"

"Yes," she said, and a slow sigh escaped from her lips. "Anthony was a drunk, Charlotte. He shouldn't have been treating patients. He was no longer as attentive to them as he needed to be. I tried to get him to take a leave of absence, to get help, but he wouldn't listen."

"If Jannie did die, then why is she coming to me? I have never seen ghosts before. I have never even believed in ghosts."

Isabella's hand slipped down my shoulder to my hand. She held it gently and said, "You are lonely, Charlotte. You're cooped up in that old house with too much time on your hands."

"But Willie . . . Willie saw her too."

Isabella's face filled with pity, and it angered me. "Willie has a great imagination," she said. "Plus, he loves his mother. He's a smart little boy. He knows what you're going through."

"No, Isabella. It doesn't make sense. I had no way of knowing about Jannie or what she looked like . . ."

With her free hand, Isabella gently pulled a stray hair from the side of my face. "Michael said you've been going to the library, that you've been doing research."

"I was there to find out about your husband . . ."

"He said you were looking at old newspaper clippings."

"Yes, about the fire, about the investigation . . ." I paused. "About you."

"There could have been a clipping about Jannie. She died only a few months before Anthony died. Maybe you saw her obituary or maybe a story about her life. Michael said she taught at the school, so maybe there was a write-up about her."

I pushed her hand away and stood up. "You think I'm making this all up? That I looked her up in the paper and am using her in some lame attempt to get attention?"

"No, Charlotte," she said, standing. "I just think—"

"Don't you think this is all just a little too coincidental?" I accused, walking toward the window, the one that faced my own house. Is this where Jannie had stood that early morning not too long ago? I thought back, but it was blurry in my mind. I couldn't concentrate.

"What do you mean, Charlotte?"

"What made you move here? What made you move into a house two doors down from a patient your husband may have killed?"

Isabella shrugged. "Charlotte, before the other morning, I had no idea about Michael or Jannie or their connection to Anthony."

I turned and looked around the family room. It looked different from inside than it looked from behind the glass of my windows. There were pictures I had never seen, pictures of Michael and Jannie and pictures of two young men, their sons. There were pictures of the four of them together, pictures of their smiling faces, faces that had not yet been marred by the darkness that sometimes comes with a new day.

"Charlotte?"

I turned toward her. "Do you think I'm stupid?"

"What?"

"Robert thinks I'm stupid. Perhaps I am. I don't know."

"Charlotte, you're speaking nonsense. You are not stupid—"

"Then tell me the truth, Isabella," I said, my voice cracking slightly. "Tell me the truth about why you live two houses down from Jannie. Tell me the truth about how your husband died."

"You know how my husband died," she whispered. Her eyes were upon me, but they had no sparkle. Isabella simply looked bewildered.

I walked around the room, absorbing the remnants of the lives that had once filled this space. "I know he died in a fire. I now know he had a patient that died too. What did her headstone say? Was it November? Yes, she died in November of last year. The fire was this past spring, back in March, right?"

Isabella didn't answer me. She didn't even move. She simply stood and stared at me with those beautiful large eyes, eyes that now looked sad and pitiful.

"So Jannie died about four months before your husband. I guess we know Jannie didn't kill Anthony," I said, laughing to myself. "After all, she was already dead according to you and Michael."

"Stop it, Charlotte. Stop this nonsense." Isabella's voice was forceful, both hurt and angry, but still she did not move. My usually animated friend was suddenly stoic.

"Oh no, Isabella. I am going to figure this thing out. You see, I think maybe Jannie has come to warn me. Maybe you did kill your husband, and she thinks I might be next. The thing I can't figure out is why you moved here. Why did you feel the need to move close to Jannie's home? Perhaps it was Michael you wanted? Had you slept with him too? Maybe you killed Jannie because you wanted her husband . . ."

Isabella shook her head, and a tear skipped down her cheek. She started to say something, but the words didn't come. She turned and headed toward the back door.

"What's the matter, Isabella? You can accuse me of being my husband's whore, of being a manipulative liar so bored with her life that she has to create imaginary friends, but you can't handle it when I have a few tough questions for you? Are you so perfect that you are above reproach?"

Isabella stopped, but she didn't immediately turn around. When she did, I could see that her eyes were wet and red. "I didn't pick this house, Charlotte. It's John's house. I had nowhere to live after the fire, so he let me stay here. I had no idea about Jannie, about her death, or about Anthony's mistakes in treating her." With that, she walked into the kitchen. I heard the back door open and close. Then I heard the faint sounds of her footsteps walking away from the house.

I wanted to chase after her, to apologize for being so cruel, but I also wanted to keep at her, to force her to explain it all to me. I was angry. I was confused. Robert had left me. Michael had left too. And now I was losing Isabella, the only person who had made an effort to brighten my days here on Wooster Street. I sat back down on the couch and dropped my head into my hands. What was happening? Was I going crazy?

I felt her before I saw her. It started as a tingling at the top of my head, like the whisper of a cold wind on a summer night. Then the sensation moved down my arms and into my hands. I turned my palms up and tried to see the energy that I now felt crawling under my skin. My hands and arms were momentarily energized, and then the feeling was gone. When I looked up, I felt her to my left, and I turned. There she was, standing by the large window, an effortless smile on her face.

She didn't say anything at first, nor did I. I was so startled by her presence that I was afraid to speak, afraid that any noise, even my own voice, might scare her away, force her to retreat.

Finally, she spoke. "Hi, Charlotte," she said, her voice still that sweet lullaby of sound.

I couldn't speak. Was she really standing there? Or was I just imagining her, like Isabella had charged?

"I'm sorry for putting you through this," she said, inching forward.

I slowly stood up from the couch. My skin went cold, causing the hairs on my arm to stand on end. "Are you real?" I heard myself whisper to her.

"That depends on what you mean," she said, her voice still soft and melodic.

"Am I imagining you?"

"No, Charlotte. I am really here."

"Why? Why are you here?"

Jannie tilted her head and put her hand to her chest. "I'm here to ask for your help."

"What do you mean?" My voice came out low, barely audible. I was breathing heavy now, and my body was shaking noticeably.

Jannie stood there for a moment contemplating her next words. She seemed solid to me, which was unsettling. It's not what I would have expected of a ghost.

"When you saw me that first time," she said. "I was surprised. I have been around this house for months, and no one, not even Michael, has seen me. It was quite nice, actually, to speak to you."

Her lips moved as she spoke, just like I recalled, but Willie was right about her words sounding in my head. I was aware of it now, how her words echoed softly in my ears as if coming from inside. But the words were spoken in her voice, not my own.

"I realized then that maybe you were the solution. Maybe you were the one who could help me . . ." She stopped suddenly and turned her head toward the kitchen. Then the smile left her face. She looked nervous. "You need to leave, Charlotte," she whispered, her words again finding their way to my head. "We'll talk another time."

"What? No, don't go," I pleaded, but already she was fading. "Jannie, come back." I reached out, but she was gone before my fingertips reached her. That's when I heard the back door open, and panic set in. I started to dash for the front door, hoping I could squeeze out before getting caught, but I wasn't quick enough. Before I could reach the front door, he called to me.

"What are you doing?" he asked, his words filled with accusation.

I stopped as soon as I heard his voice, and somehow found the courage to turn around. He stood in the archway between the kitchen and the family room. I couldn't see his face clearly, but the whites of his eyes looked ominous in the dark shadows of the room. "You scared me," I whispered.

He stared at me. I stood there, feeling awkward and foolish. "Why are you in my house?" he asked, still in the shadows of the archway.

I started to stutter an answer. "I can explain," I said, my words sounding defensive and uncertain.

"I sure hope so," he said, still motionless and waiting for me to offer him the truth.

But I couldn't do that. The truth was too bizarre, even for me. "Michael, I don't know how to say this. I don't know how to explain . . ."

Suddenly, the door burst open, and Isabella came running into the room. "I called the police, Charlotte. They should be here any minute."

"What?"

She ignored me and spoke to Michael instead. "It's a good thing for you that Charlotte heard the glass break. Otherwise, you would surely have been robbed."

Michael turned to me. "What happened, Charlotte?"

I looked at Isabella and saw her eyebrows lift. I knew that look, and I went with it. "I was on my back porch and heard glass breaking."

Isabella jumped in. "Charlotte yelled and then ran over to see what was going on. Whoever had been here was gone by the time she got to the house."

Michael took a few steps toward me. "Did you see anyone?" he asked, pushing his fingers through the fluff of hair on his head.

"No," I said, certain that my voice told the tale of my guilt. I looked again at Isabella.

"I told her she was crazy to come over here," she said, walking toward me now. She put her hand around my shoulders and gave me a half hug. "She could have been hurt."

"Why didn't you just call the cops, Charlotte?" he asked, turning on the lamps near the couch with the flip of a switch. His face was visible to me now, and he looked tired, tired and older than he had only a few days ago. I suddenly remembered my bloody hand and shoved it into my pocket.

"I don't know. I wasn't thinking. But Isabella was here. She followed me over so I wasn't alone."

"I followed you over against my better judgment," Isabella said, her arm still around me.

Michael eyed the two of us suspiciously. "Why'd you come into the house? Why didn't you just wait for the cops?"

"I don't—"

Isabella interrupted me. "We panicked. We weren't thinking. We just wanted to make sure everything was okay, that they hadn't actually made it into the house. It wasn't until we came into the house that we knew for sure that Charlotte had scared them off."

"Well that was a very stupid thing to do," he said. "You both could have been hurt."

"When I heard you coming in, I panicked," I said. "I thought you might be one of them."

"So that's why you were running for the front door?" he asked. There was still a hint of skepticism in his voice.

Isabella laughed and hugged me tighter. "Oh, Charlotte. You must have been so scared."

I laughed uncomfortably. Then there was a quick knock on the back door. "Is everything all right in here?" the voice asked. Isabella winked at me, and I knew at once that it was Officer Lucarelli.

Michael walked back into the kitchen. We could hear them talking. Isabella leaned over and whispered, "Don't worry. John will handle this. You're lucky he was in the neighborhood."

"I'm sorry about before," I whispered back.

Isabella smiled and squeezed my shoulder, but the pain was still evident in her expression. "Come on," she said, and together we walked into the kitchen.

Officer Lucarelli listened to our story and took notes of all we had to say. Then he wrote up a report and had us both review it. I knew that report would never make it to the police station, that this was all a show for Michael Spain, and the guilt overwhelmed me. But how could I explain myself otherwise? How could I possibly tell Michael that I broke into his house in search of his dead wife? And how could I possibly tell him that I had actually found her there?

Chapter 29

*I*sabella walked back to the police cruiser with Officer Lucarelli, leaving me waiting at the back end of the driveway with Michael. He had been quiet most of the night, allowing Isabella and I to talk and tell our stories. I had no idea whether he believed us or not, but he did not offer up any accusations.

After a few uncomfortable moments, I finally found the courage to ask him where he'd been the past few days.

"I went to Boston and spent some time with my son," he said, but he did not look at me.

"Is everything okay?" I asked, not sure exactly what I meant.

Michael turned to me then. "Paul thinks I should stay away from you, that you are not being truthful."

I felt my stomach drop, but it did not stop me from defending myself. "So you told him I saw Jannie?"

He didn't answer me at first. He just stood there, staring into the darkness, seeming to contemplate all that life had left at his feet. "I told him what you told me. He wasn't very receptive to it."

"What about your other son?" I asked. "Did you talk to him about it too?"

Michael shook his head. "No, we have . . . well, we don't talk as much."

"Why not?"

Michael breathed in the fresh summer air and lifted his eyes to the stars. "Because he can't forgive me."

"Forgive you?"

"For letting his mother get treated by a drunk. For letting her die."

"That wasn't your fault," I said. I wanted to touch him, to offer my support, but I feared him just enough to hesitate. It wasn't a physical fear, not the type of fear that you feel for a stranger. It was an emotional fear, a fear I couldn't yet define or fully comprehend, a fear that made me resist my temptation to open my soul to him.

Michael still didn't look at me, but I could see the shadow of darkness in his eyes, a shadow that spoke of the demons still haunting him. "So Isabella told you? She told you about her drunken husband?"

I walked closer to him and reached out long enough to touch his arm momentarily. It was an awkward gesture. I wanted to do more. I wanted to hold him and tell him it would be okay, but I couldn't.

"Yes, she told me," I said. "You can't blame yourself, Michael. You obviously loved your wife and tried to help her."

When he finally looked up at me, his eyes were red and misty. "But I was stupid. I was stupid to let that happen to her, to let him kill her. And for that, I can never forgive myself."

"There is nothing to forgive. From what Isabella has told me of her husband, he was a great oncologist, at least until—"

"Until he became an alcoholic?"

"How could you possibly have known that?"

"I should have made sure they were monitoring her. I should have asked more questions. I should have done my own research. That's what everyone always says, right? That you have to be your own doctor. But instead I left her in their hands, in his hands. I gave him all of my trust, and he pissed on it. He poisoned her, and I stood by and watched it happen."

Michael turned away and started to walk down the driveway toward the street, just as Isabella was returning. I started to follow him, but Isabella grabbed my arm. "Let him go," she said.

"But I need to tell him the truth."

"What truth?"

"He needs to know about Jannie. He needs to know that she's still with him."

"Charlotte, if you keep talking to him about his dead wife, he is going to lose it. Can't you see what he's going through?"

I looked into her mascara-laden eyes. "You still don't believe I've seen her, do you?"

Isabella pouted her lips. "I'm just not a big believer in ghosts, Charlotte."

It struck me that Isabella had lost her husband four months after Michael had lost Jannie, making her loss even more recent than his, yet she was getting on with her life. She even had a boyfriend, a boyfriend who existed before her husband's death. Isabella was surviving, but Michael was so distraught by his loss that he could barely breathe. Why was her loss more bearable than his? Why wasn't I seeing Anthony in Isabella's windows?

"She came to me again," I said, keeping my eyes on her. I knew I was inviting conflict by raising this subject with her, but that fact only seemed to motivate me more.

"What do you mean?" she asked.

"After you left, she came to me. She wants me to help her."

Isabella shook her head in disbelief, but she didn't allow her skepticism to turn ugly like it had earlier. Instead, she took the opportunity to tease me. "Did she tell you I killed her?"

"I didn't mean that."

A slight smile rose from her lips. "Yes, you did. At least a little bit."

I shrugged. "Maybe a little bit. Listen, I have to check on Willie. You want to come inside and talk?"

There was breeze, and the slight chill made Isabella hug herself for warmth. "It might be a good idea for us to finish this conversation. I wouldn't want you to go to sleep tonight thinking that I killed more than one person."

It took me a second to register what she had said. "Just because Robert thinks you killed your husband doesn't mean I do."

"*Do you* think I killed Anthony?"

"I don't know, Isabella," I said. "Maybe you can clear that up for me over a drink or two."

Before we left the Spains' yard, I glanced down the driveway to where Michael was standing. I could only see the outline of his body in the darkness of the summer night, but I felt his pain as if it were my own. I had to resist the urge to turn around, to run to him and offer him a shoulder. I was confused by my interest in him and his circumstances and very much troubled by the obsessive behavior I had earlier engaged in. Something was driving me to Michael and his house, making me do things I would never have envisioned doing only days ago. My world was changing, spinning beneath my feet, and there was nothing I could do to stop it. I knew that my life on Wooster Street would never be the same, that I would never be the same. This was a truth I was certain of, and the odd thing about it was that it had very little to do with whether or not Robert came back into my life.

Chapter 30

After checking on Willie, I poured two glasses of wine and handed one to Isabella. When we sat down at the kitchen table, I engaged her instantly, not wanting any period of silence to steal my courage. I needed answers tonight. I feared I would never sleep again without them.

"So tell me about jail," I said, knowing I would have to ease her into the conversation about her husband's death.

"What's there to tell?" she said, sipping at her wine. "It's a horrible place, not somewhere I would ever have imagined myself."

"Why did it take so long for the bail money to come through?"

"My family doesn't have a lot of money, Charlotte. They are hardworking people barely getting by. It wasn't easy for them to come up with such a large amount." Isabella laughed, but it was a sorrowful laugh, not a joyous one. "They probably didn't want to send it. I'm not the most beloved daughter after all. I am what you call the black sheep of the family. The girl who's always getting herself into trouble at everyone else's expense."

"Seems like I may be following in your footsteps," I said, and my mind instantly returned to the insanity I had experienced earlier.

"I am worried about you, Charlotte. Perhaps I am a bad influence on you like Robbie said. Speaking of the devil, have you heard from him?"

"No, he hasn't called. But he took most of our savings out of the bank, leaving me with just enough money in the checking account to pay our bills and get groceries."

"How nice of him. Hasn't he even called to speak to Willie?"

"Nope." It surprised me how detached I felt, how my mind was more focused on Michael and Jannie than it was on Robert and his disappearance. Perhaps it was because I knew he was with *her*. I didn't know her name, didn't really care to, but I knew he was not alone. Somehow that reality didn't hurt me now as much as I would have expected it to. "But enough about me. Tell me what's going on with your case."

"Well, my attorney is working with an investigator to prove it wasn't arson. From what I'm told, there's a lot of really bad science out there, and the people from the insurance company and the fire department are relying on that bad science to show my guilt."

"So do you think you will get off?"

Isabella sipped at her wine, let it swirl in her mouth, and then swallowed it slowly. "I don't know," she said, speaking more to herself than to me. "Perhaps I don't deserve to."

"What do you mean?" My heart raced. She had finally opened the door.

Isabella tilted her head and rubbed at her neck. Her fingers were manicured, but the nail polish had worn away in spots, and several of her nails looked chipped.

"I wanted to kill him, Charlotte. I had actually thought about it. But when I left Anthony that night, it wasn't *his* death I was thinking about."

It was a quiet night, so quiet that I could hear my own breath as I waited for her to finish. When she didn't say anything more, I asked, "Whose death were you thinking about?"

She looked at me, and her eyes darkened. "Anthony was drinking. He was wild, out of control. I had never seen him that bad." She took a long drink of wine and then replenished her glass. "He told me he wanted a divorce because he was in love with the whore."

She stopped herself and took a deep breath. A tear skipped down her cheek. "I was stunned. It was bad enough that he had been cheating on me, that wasn't a shock to me, but when he told me it was Marissa, I went numb."

"Marissa?"

"She was a nurse that he worked with. I knew her. I thought we were friends. I had even been to her house. I was so stupid."

"Marissa is the whore?"

Isabella smiled faintly. "Yes. It's easier to call her the whore. When I think of her as Marissa, I think of her as my friend, the friend who totally betrayed me."

"You never suspected?"

"No. I knew Anthony was cheating on me. That had been obvious for quite some time. That's really what drove me to John in the first place.

But Marissa and I had been close. I had opened up to her. I had trusted her." Her voice broke off, and she struggled to regain her composure.

"When he told me it was Marissa, I slapped him. I was so angry. It was a hard slap, so hard that he dropped his scotch. It poured all over the sofa." I could see the anguish in her face and knew that the memories of that night were tormenting her. She fought to finish her story, her lower lip now trembling. "That's when he hit me. Right in the face. He knocked me down. It was horrible. I still can't believe he did it."

"I'm so sorry, Isabella."

"I was angry, Charlotte. I was distraught. Crazy. So crazy. I told him I was going to kill her. I was screaming. I don't remember everything I said, but I was out of control. I knew where Marissa lived. It wasn't very far away. I had been there many times before."

"What did you do?"

Isabella looked at me, her face wet, her eyes dull and sad as if all the happiness of her life had washed away with her tears. "I was going to kill her, Charlotte. That's all I could think about. I grabbed Anthony's handgun from the bedroom and ran out of the house. He tried to stop me, but he had been drinking so much he could barely walk, never mind catch a crazed woman."

She flew her head back and let out a deep sigh. Then Isabella closed her eyes, her face angled toward the ceiling, and shook her head in apparent disbelief. Her body began to shake. She leaned forward and grabbed hold of the wineglass with both hands, trying to steady herself with its grip. It didn't work. Her hands still trembled, and she eventually had to let go of the goblet. That's when she stood up and walked toward the back door. She didn't leave, but she didn't turn and face me either. She finished her story with her back to me, trembling as she spoke of the night that still haunted her.

"He must have called her because she wasn't there when I arrived. I went into her house with every intention of killing her. I really think I would have done it too. I was that angry, that insane. Within a matter of only a few minutes, I made a mess of her house, knocked over her precious vases and figurines, threw her lamps to the floor. I destroyed the place, screaming vulgarities with every toss and kick." Her breathing was heavy, and her words came out with a breathy force.

"What did you do next?" I asked, still in my seat at the kitchen table. I was so hypnotized by her tale that I hadn't yet touched my wine.

"I worried that she had gone to my house, that she had gone to be with Anthony. So I rushed back." Her voice caught, and she stood in silence for a long time. When she finally turned to me, the distress in her face was evident. Her anguish ran deep, overwhelming the beauty of her features and draining the color from her olive skin. She actually appeared older than she had only minutes before.

"When I got home, Marissa wasn't there. But Anthony was there and . . ." She eyed me reluctantly. It was as if she knew that what she was about to say would forever change how I saw her, would forever change what I felt when I looked into her eyes. Warily she continued, "The house was already on fire. My instinct should have been to run inside, to see if Anthony was still in there. But I didn't do that. Instead, I stood on the back lawn. I stood in the grass and stared at the fire and smoke. I can remember walking to the picture window and looking through the glass. He was just lying there on the floor, motionless, the fire and smoke all around him. I felt nothing. There was no sense of urgency. I stood there in the grass looking through the window as the flames reached higher and higher. I knew he was helpless. I knew he would not get out of there on his own." She gasped at the memory and instinctively pulled her hand to her mouth. "But I did nothing. I just stood there and watched him die."

She was looking in my direction now, but her eyes did not see me. I could tell by her glassy look and empty stare that her eyes saw only what they had seen that night. With her body still trembling, her voice lowered to a whisper, she said, "I just stood there looking through the window."

I stood and approached her. "You were in shock, Isabella."

"No, Charlotte. I chose not to save him. I chose to let him die for what he had done to me." Her hands were still at her mouth. Streaks of mascara ran down her face, and her lipstick was smudged against her wet skin. "I should have gone inside. I should have done something."

"Maybe he was already dead, Isabella," I offered, not knowing what to say, not knowing what to think. My instinct was to protect her, to save her from her own guilt. "I've read that most fire victims die of asphyxiation before the fire ever actually touches them."

She looked at me with such intensity that I knew there was more, more than she had already divulged. Perhaps it was the way her eyes offered an apology before her lips could tremble out the words. Perhaps it was the way she tilted her head, the same way a child tilts her head before confessing to a youthful sin. Whatever it was, I knew instantly that a confession of much greater magnitude was about to slip from her lips.

Just as the words began to pour out, just when I thought she might explain what else was tormenting her, the phone rang.

"It's Robert," I said, reading the caller ID. He was calling from his cell phone.

"You should answer it," Isabella said.

"He can leave a message."

"It's okay, Charlotte. Talk to him."

"I'll call him back later," I said, just as the answering machine clicked on.

"Charlotte, it's Robert," he said, his voice flat and businesslike. "You're probably in bed. I'm coming over in the morning. I'd like to see William, and we need to talk. I'll be there at nine." With that, he hung up.

"Well, at least he finally called," Isabella said, her voice still unsteady.

"I can only imagine what he wants to talk about," I said, trying to suppress the anxiety now building inside. I turned to her. "It's not important. I'll deal with him tomorrow."

Isabella's face was stained with her makeup, but she did not notice or care. She had regained some of her composure and seemed content on leaving her tale where it had ended. She wiped her face with her hands and fluttered her eyes in an effort to clear her vision. "Do you want me to stay with you tonight?"

"No. I'll be fine. But I would like to finish our talk."

"I can come back in the morning. I'm not afraid of him."

"No, it's okay. Let's forget about Robert for now." I took her hands in mine and held them tight. "Tell me the rest."

Isabella offered me a faint smile, but there was only sorrow in her expression. "I can't," she whispered. "I'm sorry."

Isabella quickly put herself around my shoulders and held me tight. "You are a good friend, Charlotte," she whispered. "Thank you for listening."

I kept her in my grip when she loosened her own, "You can trust me, Isabella. You don't have to leave."

Isabella pushed herself away and dropped her eyes to the floor. "I'm sorry, Charlotte. I really have to go." She glanced up at me momentarily and then turned for the door. She opened the screen, hesitated, and looked back at me one last time. "All you need to know, Charlotte, is that I didn't start that fire, but I might have been able to save Anthony, and I chose not to."

"You were scared. You didn't know what you were doing," I said, trying to offer her some comfort.

"No, Charlotte. I knew. Remember that when you sit down with Robbie tomorrow morning. Don't let yourself get to that ugly place. You still have a chance to save your soul."

With that, she turned and left. The screen door creaked as it floated shut against the doorjamb. I sat and finished the bottle of wine alone, my head filled with her words and thoughts of what I had already become.

Chapter 31

I fell asleep quickly that night, exhausted from the day's events and tipsy from the wine. As I drifted off, my mind filled with images of Michael, Jannie, and their two sons. I had never met the boys, but I had seen their framed photos, and their faces stayed with me.

Jannie was sitting in the rocker on the back porch again, just like she had been that first day I saw her. Only this time she wasn't sitting in the shade. She was sitting in the full sun, her older boy, also named Michael, sitting beside her. They were deep in conversation, but I lost the first few words to the sounds of the birds at the feeder on the lawn.

I felt myself being pulled closer as if I was edging over the fence and into their yard with the whisper of wind in the air. I could actually feel the heat of the sun on my face and back as I neared them. They did not know I was there, but I was close enough to see that she had already lost quite a bit of weight and much of her hair from the chemotherapy. Her son was handsome, but his good looks did not hide the worry in his face as he spoke to her.

"I can stay here, Mom. It's not a problem. I've already spoken to my boss, and he understands that I may need to take a leave of absence."

"No, Michael. I don't want you to do that. Your father is here with me, and that's all I need."

"I'm worried about you. I want to help."

"Thank you, sweetie. It's good to know that you are there for me if I need it, but I'm okay for now." She didn't speak as softly as I was used to. Her words came slower and with more effort, and there was no precise beginning and end to her consonants and vowels.

Michael took her hand and gently rubbed the skin of her fingers. "Is it painful?"

"The chemo?" she asked, and he nodded.

"Not painful really. But it kicks the shit out of you."

They both laughed. Somehow I knew that Jannie was not one to swear, and the sound of that word coming from her otherwise cautious lips made even me smile.

"Are you scared?" he asked.

She smiled at him and put her other hand on top of his so that their hands formed a small stack. "A little. I'm not really afraid of dying. I'm more afraid of leaving your father, of leaving you boys."

He weakened at the thought, and his eyes teared up. His mouth tightened, and he labored to hold back the emotions that fought to break through.

"It's okay, Michael. Everything is going to be okay. God has a plan for all of us, and we have to trust that he knows what he's doing."

The wind picked up a bit, and her thinning hair rose and fell with the breeze that blew across the porch.

"You should go inside, Mom. It's getting a bit chilly out here."

"You know how I love to be outside, Michael. I can't stand sitting in the house when the sun is so shiny and bright in the sky."

"You can still see the sun through the windows. You just won't be as cold." He reached behind her and pulled her sweater up around her shoulders.

"It's depressing looking at the world through a window," she whispered. "I want to experience the sun firsthand, not through a pane of glass."

He nodded and continued to caress her hands. "What if God's plan is to take you away from us?" he asked, and again he grimaced.

"Then we must accept it. We must trust in his choice for us." She didn't look at him when she spoke this time. Instead, she lifted her chin upward and let the sun grace her face with its bright heat. She was smiling despite the aches and pains in her body.

Michael shifted in his chair uncomfortably. He let go of her hands and stood. Then he walked toward the rail of the porch and looked out across the yard. "Dad says you haven't been sleeping well, that you've been getting sick a lot."

She nodded, her chin still lifted, her eyes closed in the glare of the sun. "It's part of the process. They warned me I might get quite ill. When you go through chemo, it kills the good along with the bad, so you have to suffer a little before you can get better." She took a slow breath and continued, "You know, since we moved into this house all those years ago, I have always enjoyed sitting on this porch. There is something about being here that brings me peace and joy. Even when I am sick from the chemo, I feel better here for some reason."

"That's good, Mom." His voice was lower now, sadder.

She laughed to herself. "I used to think how nice it would be to have a porch on the second floor so I could be closer to the sky. Your father used to joke that if I had my way, I'd have a rocker on the roof so I could see all of God's glory from way up there."

"I remember him joking about that," Michael whispered. He was leaning with his back against the railing now, his hands gripped on the wood as if he was afraid to let go.

Jannie was still smiling from the memory. "He was joking, but he was right. I used to fantasize about how nice it would be to sit on the roof and look out across the valley. What a beautiful sight it must be from up there."

"Maybe when you get better, we'll find a way to get you up there."

She looked at him knowingly, and I sensed that she knew, that she knew she would not get better, that she would not survive this, that she would not be able to fulfill his wish of having her be a grandmother to his unborn children. "If I don't get better," she said, "look for me on the roof because that's where my soul will go."

"Don't say that, Mom," he pleaded. "You will get better."

"But if I don't, Michael," she said, her voice suddenly somber, "I will be okay. I know that. I will be okay because I will be in a better place, a place where I can see the beauty of the world at every turn."

His head dropped, and I instantly felt his sorrow. "How will I know?"

"Know what?"

"How will I know you're okay?" His voice was unsteady, and he wiped at his eyes.

Jannie struggled to stand, not an easy feat for a woman so fragile and weak. But she managed her way to him and whispered in his ear, "Somehow I will let you know that I'm okay." She took a deep breath and rested her head against his chest. "Somehow I will show you that I am happy, that I am at peace."

"But how?"

She smiled and caressed his face. "I will tell you about the view, how there is no need to look through windows to see the beauty of the world."

Chapter 32

The next morning, I vividly remembered the dream of Jannie and her son Michael. I wondered whether it was just a dream, a justification for her presence on the roof. It seemed so real, the kind of dream that sticks with you because it doesn't seem like a dream at all. I was still thinking about it when Robert walked in the back door at 9:00 a.m. sharp, just as he promised. It bothered me that he walked in without knocking as if nothing had happened, as if I still had no rights of privacy in his presence despite his betrayal.

"Where's your friend?" he asked with his usual smug look.

"What do you want to talk about, Robert?"

"Where's William?" he asked, walking past me into the family room.

"He's upstairs playing," I said, following him. "You can talk to him later."

He turned to me. "I'm here to make you a deal."

Robert sat down on the couch and spread his arms high along its back. I said nothing and waited for him to explain.

"This obviously isn't working out for either one of us," he said, his eyes drifting a bit.

"That's pretty apparent," I whispered. The hurt that had eluded me these last few days now came rushing in.

He cleared his throat and said, "I'd like a divorce. It'll be the best thing for both of us."

I didn't immediately react, at least not verbally. Part of me already knew my marriage was over, that it had been over for quite some time. But another part of me, a part I didn't quite understand, clung to the vision of how my life was supposed to be; and divorce simply was not part of that picture. Even after all Robert had done, after all he had *not* done, it still hurt that he didn't want me in his life anymore. It felt like I had failed somehow.

"Charlotte, did you hear what I said?"

"I heard you."

"We don't need to make this difficult. It's important that we handle this maturely, especially for William's sake."

I was taken aback by his cavalier approach to the end of our marriage and troubled by his use of Willie as a sword against me. But when I saw Robert's face and the way he looked at me, in that uncaring and emotionless way that made me feel so diminutive, I suddenly realized that my life might actually be better without him in it. The possibility of not living under the weight of his distance and detachment entered my consciousness, and this alone caused a wave of calm to push away the hurt and anger I was feeling. It was unexpected and surprising, but suddenly I felt very empowered.

"I'll sign over the house, but we'll have to refinance so you can take over the mortgage," he offered. "We'll split the credit cards. There's not much on them anyway. We'll each keep our own cars and be responsible for our own loans. We'll share custody of William. I'll take him every other weekend and want free visitation during the week. I'm sure we can work that out. We'll alternate holidays and in the summers, I'd like two straight weeks with him in addition to my alternate weekends and weekly visits."

He stayed where he was on the couch, his arms spread so wide that I could see the veins pulsating in his arms as he spoke.

"I'll live in this house with Willie, but you'll keep paying the mortgage," I said. "No bank is going to let me finance the mortgage on my own given that I haven't worked outside our home since Willie was born, a circumstance you demanded. I'll pay for my own car, but you'll pay alimony and child support. You'll also give me the $8,000 I'm going to need to retain a divorce attorney. I believe that was the retainer your friend Joe had to pay when he went through his divorce, right? It's a good thing I actually listened when you spoke to me, a favor you didn't often return. You'll also pay off the credit cards with the savings you stole from our bank accounts. Our remaining assets will be divided equally, including your 401(k). As far as Willie, I'll have primary custody. You can have weekday visits when I allow it. I'll agree to the alternate weekends and two weeks in the summer, but you'll pay for his summer camps."

For the first time in a really long time, Robert actually looked stunned. He stared at me, seemingly speechless, before he snapped back to the lawyer-husband he had been for so long now. "What makes you think you can dictate how this is going to play out?"

"This isn't about dictation, Robert. It's about what's best for all of us, especially Willie, remember?"

"If you choose to make this difficult, Charlotte, you'll have to find a lawyer on your own, and you certainly don't have the money it will take to find a good one. I'll have you buried in so much paperwork and attorney's fees, you'll never find your way out."

Isabella had taught me many things over the past summer, but I didn't fully realize how much I had learned until that moment. "I'm not afraid of a fight, Robert. I saw this coming a long time ago and am well-prepared for one. If you really want a fight, get ready for a criminal action as well as a civil suit against both you and your girlfriend. Adultery is a felony in the state of Massachusetts, punishable by up to three years in prison. Won't you lose your license to practice law if you get convicted of a felony?" He stared at me, his anger obvious, but he did not respond. "If you think I won't be able to prove it, think again. I've been on to you and your girlfriend for some time now and have plenty of proof to make my case, so much proof in fact that I am sure a civil attorney will gladly take my case on retainer just to get the free publicity. The question you need to answer is whether that's the way you want this to play out."

I had no money, of course, and no proof that he had cheated on me. But he didn't know that, and I wasn't lying about Massachusetts law. I actually knew, based on conversations I had with Isabella, that it was one of the few states with an adultery statute. It was rarely enforced, but it was still on the books, and at least one jilted wife had gotten quite a hefty judgment against her straying husband and his ill-fated secretary based on their adulterous acts and the injuries and damages such behavior had caused her. Surely, Robert would know I was right on that point.

Robert was angry, but he also looked bewildered. He stood up without a further word and headed for the back door. He yanked open the screen door and then slammed it shut. I could actually hear him as he stormed down the driveway, his sneakers flapping loudly against the pavement, before he kicked his car into reverse and made his departure known to every neighbor on Wooster Street.

He never did say hello to his own son. And while I felt for Willie and worried about his father's abandonment of him, I couldn't help but smile.

I had finally conquered Robert, even if only momentarily. He would be back. He wouldn't give up that easily. But I had shown him that I would be a force to reckon with, not the weak-minded wife he had expected.

Several hours passed before Isabella made her way over to the house, a large envelope in her hand. "I saw the jerk drive off earlier. He seemed quite mad. Is everything okay?"

"He wants a divorce and was trying to dictate the terms."

"And?"

"And it was great, Isabella. I finally felt like I was in control. I finally stood up to him. I think I have you to thank for that."

Isabella smiled. "Well, what do you know. Our little Charlotte is finally growing up."

"It's not over yet, but I am going to enjoy this while I can. I'm worried about Willie and how this will affect him, but I honestly think he'll be okay with it, so long as Robert and I don't get too nasty with each other."

"And you're okay with the divorce."

"I was upset initially but, surprisingly, okay with it as soon as I realized it was for the best. I have no idea what I'll do, how I'll make any money, how I'll support myself and Willie. But I am going to try really hard not to get too overwhelmed and stressed by it all. With everything else that is going on, it should be easier to put this in perspective."

Isabella approached and gave me a long hug. "I'm sorry."

I hugged her back and then asked, "What's in the envelope?"

"My lawyer dropped this off this morning. It's an expert report on the cause of the fire. I thought you might like to see it. Maybe it will ease your mind a little." She smiled at me and handed over the envelope.

I wanted to tell her that I didn't need to see the report, that I trusted her, but the truth was that I wanted proof. I wanted some assurance of her innocence. So I took hold of the envelope and opened it up. Inside was a large typed report, nearly twenty pages in length with single-spaced sentences. Much of it was too scientific for me to fully understand, but there were a few crucial points that were highlighted and emphasized throughout the report. These key points were summarized in layman's terms, terms I could understand and appreciate, terms that brought me comfort and reassurance that Isabella might actually be innocent after all, at least of starting the fire in the first place.

The report first challenged the insurance investigator's reliance on the "burn pattern" on the floor as evidence that a gasoline accelerant was poured there to start the fire. According to Isabella's expert, reading burn patterns is like reading tea leaves. He noted several times in the report that flashover—explained as the transition phase between free burning and full room involvement—causes burn patterns on floors that are often confused with liquid pour patterns.

In fact, he claimed that there was no evidence of any accelerant being used to start the fire. Although gasoline was found in the floorboards in the area of the couch, it was a lead-based gasoline, a product commonly used decades ago but rarely used today. This leaded gasoline was even found in areas of the house that were untouched by the fire. Apparently, the insurance investigator had not thought to test the gasoline for the presence of lead and had therefore missed this key piece of evidence.

Isabella's expert surmised that the gasoline found in the floorboards was likely residue from the floor varnish commonly used on hard woods when the house was first built. This conclusion was further supported by the fact that while gasoline was found in the floorboards beneath the carpet, no gasoline was actually detected in the synthetic pile carpet or in the carpet pad on top of the floor, another key point that the insurance investigator failed to highlight.

According to Isabella's expert, if gasoline had been poured on the floor where the "burn pattern" was located, as concluded by the insurance investigator, the furniture in that area would display evidence of a low burn. Although all the furniture in the room had been destroyed by the fire department before Isabella's defense team had a chance to do any analysis of it, Isabella's expert had gained access to photos of the fire scene. These photos showed that the front lower portion of the couch and love seat were not severely burned. In fact, the end table was burned more on the side facing the couch than on the front, again indicating that the fire started on the couch rather than on the floor. The expert concluded that the newspaper and blanket on the couch, combined with the spilled alcohol from Anthony's drink, served as an accelerant, rather than any gasoline on the floor.

What surprised me the most, however, was the section of the report detailing the speed with which a fire can accelerate and incapacitate its victims. According to the expert, within ninety seconds the fire could have started and spread toward the ceiling. Within two and a half to three minutes, the smoke and hot gases would have been enough to slow down a person trying to escape. Within four minutes, the combination of the heat and carbon monoxide could have caused Anthony to lose consciousness. Within six minutes, he could have been dead from carbon monoxide poisoning.

The expert hypothesized that flashover occurred within those crucial six minutes, that within six minutes of the start of the fire, the entire room was consumed. He highlighted the fact that the windows in the family room had been open due to the warm spring, which helped fuel the fire. He also emphasized that once a flaming fire has started in a piece of modern upholstered furniture, like the Capellos' couch, the fire would have burned rapidly.

Based on Anthony's autopsy report, which indicated that he had a blood alcohol content of 0.18 percent and a carbon monoxide level of about 45 percent, Isabella's expert concluded that Anthony died from carbon monoxide poisoning and that his death was an unfortunate accident, caused by his own negligence and poor judgment. He hypothesized that Anthony accidentally started the fire when he lit up a cigar and dropped it onto the upholstered couch, a couch that had already been drenched with scotch (based on Isabella's statements). The autopsy report showed that Anthony's palms had been burned, which indicated he tried to pat out the fire with his bare hands. The expert further hypothesized that since Anthony was drunk, as indicated by his blood alcohol content, he may have tried to put out the fire with the newspaper or a blanket, both of which were found burned on the couch in the family room. This act could have caused the fire to spread even more rapidly.

A burnt pitcher found near the couch suggested that Anthony made an effort to pour water on the fire. There was also an empty fire extinguisher on the floor by his body, a fire extinguisher that Isabella swore had been hung on the wall of the basement stairwell, which meant Anthony had stumbled his way around the house while the fire was spreading. All of this confirmed that Anthony simply stayed in the house too long, wasting precious time and trying to put out a fire that was beyond his control. The combination of alcohol and carbon monoxide incapacitated him so quickly that he had no chance of escape after the passage of about four minutes. He was dead long before the fire department came and extinguished the fire. He was dead even though the fire never consumed his body.

By now, I was sitting at the kitchen table, my eyes glued to the words of the report. I felt Isabella's presence in the chair to my right, but she let me read in quiet. When I had finished, I looked up and found her staring back at me.

"Have the prosecutors seen this?" I asked.

"They were supposed to get it today."

"This is pretty compelling data," I said. "I'm shocked frankly that the insurance investigator overlooked so much. How can that be?"

"From what my expert says, it happens all the time." Isabella seemed happy about the report, maybe even a little hopeful, but there was an emptiness in her eyes that left me feeling uneasy.

"Is everything okay, Isabella?"

She laughed at me. "I suppose things could be better, don't you?"

I smiled and acknowledged the absurdity of my question. "It's just that . . . well, I thought maybe there was something more you wanted to talk about yesterday before Robert called."

Isabella reached over and grabbed the report. "I think this says it all."

"I do believe you, you know. And I'm sorry for what I said before, what I said when we were in Michael's house."

"It's okay, Charlotte. You're dealing with a bunch of garbage yourself these days. We're all a bit confused."

I nodded in agreement. "Thanks for sharing that with me. I think this just might be your ticket to freedom. Maybe you will get that insurance money after all."

"Maybe," she whispered and tilted her head. "But I'm sure they'll have their own expert with his own view of things. You know how that works."

"I just don't know how they can say that you poured gasoline on the floor and started the fire if there is no gasoline in the carpet. And the presence of lead in the gas found in the floorboards all but rules out the possibility that the gas was put there at the time of the fire."

"They'll probably just come up with some new theory to tag me with guilt. Maybe they'll say now that I started the fire on the couch, with a mixture of scotch and rolled-up newspapers. Who knows. I've been dealing with this for so long I simply have no faith in the system anymore."

"I'm sorry, Isabella. Is there anything I can do?"

She reached out her hand and briefly touched my shoulder. "Just be my friend, Charlotte. That's what I need the most right now."

I gave her a big hug and whispered, "I will always be there for you, Isabella. Always."

Chapter 33

Thankfully, Willie had a playdate later that afternoon, something I had arranged earlier in the week. I dropped him off at his friend's house, shared a few minutes of conversation with the friend's mom, who remained ignorant of my marital strife, and then I headed back home. The entire way I thought of Michael and Jannie. I cringed at the pain he must have felt when she died. I wondered whether he spent his days thinking of the possibilities that never came to pass. Did he sit in that house by himself thinking about her and where she was? Did he torment himself with thoughts of what he could have done differently to create an alternate outcome, an outcome that kept her alive and by his side when the sun went down at night?

I couldn't get Michael Spain out of my mind, and that alone caused me endless confusion. Why was I so obsessed with him and his dead wife? I had never felt such an emotional pull before, and it troubled me. Were my feelings for him simply born of neighborly concern, or was I feeling something more? And if my emotions for him were anything but the innocent concern of one human being for another, what did that mean? Why would I feel such things for someone I barely knew? And what about Jannie? Was she showing herself to me because she knew that I was a lonely woman on the verge of divorce? Was she afraid I might be developing an interest in her husband? No, that couldn't be it. She didn't fear me. She wanted my help. But my help for what?

So many thoughts coursed through my mind that by the time I pulled into the driveway, I had no idea how I had gotten there. I had no memory of the trip home. I sat in my car for several long minutes, staring over my own front yard at the Spains' porch. I had to talk to him again. I had to make sure he knew I was his friend, that I could help him. Is that what Jannie wanted me to do? Did she want me to help him survive his loss?

But why me? How could I possibly help him when my own life was in such a shambles?

I nervously walked to his front porch and up the steps. I had butterflies in my stomach, a sensation I hadn't felt in years. I hesitantly rang the doorbell without any idea of what I would say if he actually came to the door. I knew he was inside. Something told me he was home. I could actually feel his heartbreak as I stood and waited for him to answer. When I heard him grab the knob from the other side and start to pull the door open, I suddenly panicked. What would I say to him? Why was I even here?

He pulled the door open. When his eyes met mine, my heart began to thump even harder. "Hi," he said.

"Hi," I answered, fearful that he could see the beating of my chest against the shirt I was wearing.

"Is everything all right?" he asked. He was in a pair of shorts and a T-shirt, and his hair was messed up, like he had just awoken from sleep.

I stuttered a bit and then asked him if he had time for a quick chat. He motioned me in. We walked silently through the front room toward the back of the house. "We can sit in the kitchen," he said, still walking, his back to me.

He pulled out a chair and motioned me to it. He sat down and looked at me curiously, but he did not speak. He looked tired, restless.

My hands were trembling inexplicably, and my breath caught a bit as I spoke. "I'm sorry about yesterday," I started. "We shouldn't have come in your house . . . at least not before the police arrived."

"Well, I'm just glad nothing happened." He was somewhat distant and distracted, but he didn't seem angry.

"I wanted to talk to you about Jannie," I said, still not completely sure what I would say.

Michael fidgeted. "I don't know, Charlotte. It's not an easy thing for me to talk about."

"I know and I'm sorry. I just feel like we should talk about her, about what I've seen. I don't want to hurt you. I hope you know that."

He scratched at his eyebrow. "I know. I just don't think you understand."

"Maybe you can help me understand."

"She used to sit on the porch all the time, even after she got sick. So when you told me how you saw her there in the rocker, I didn't know what to think."

"I know," I said.

"And then you said she was sitting in the corner in the shade . . ." He stopped himself and paused a moment as if to regain his courage before continuing, "She loved the sun, but toward the end, she had no choice but to sit in the shade. She was so . . ."

He couldn't finish his sentence. He stood and walked over to the counter. "Would you like something to drink? Coffee or water?"

"No, thanks. Michael, there's something I didn't tell you." I thought back to my dream. It had stayed with me all day.

He turned and rubbed at his face. "I don't know if we should keep talking about this, Charlotte. It confuses me. It's upsetting." He was rubbing at his neck now, the pain evident in his face.

"I'm really not trying to upset you, Michael," I said.

"I just think I need more time. Every time I think of her, every time I hear her name, I ache inside."

"But I feel like I need to tell you something."

"My son thinks we should . . . well, that we should keep a distance."

Panic set in. "No, that's not what she wants."

"Who?"

"I don't know. I don't know what I'm saying."

"Charlotte, this is too much for me."

"But I need to tell you," I said and then unexpectedly started to cry. I was at once overwhelmed and embarrassed. I had no idea where these emotions were coming from.

He approached me but stopped before he came too close. "What's the matter?"

I held my head in my hands and tried to regain my composure. "I'm sorry," I whimpered. "I didn't mean to do this."

"Charlotte, what is it?"

The truth was that I couldn't answer him, not only because of the weight of the grief I now felt, but because I didn't fully comprehend my own feelings. I could only surmise that the visions of Jannie and the realization of her death, combined with the odd emotional attachment I felt to Michael, had driven me to a state of despair and uncertainty. It certainly didn't help that my best friend was at risk of imprisonment and my own husband now wanted a divorce. Perhaps I was simply falling apart.

"Charlotte?" he persisted.

The words came out so suddenly and without conscious thought that I didn't even realize what I had said until I saw the look of astonishment on his face.

"What?" he stammered.

I choked on the lump in my throat. What was I doing? Why was I telling him this?

"Charlotte, what did you just say?"

I let out a choked cry and repeated the words, "Willie saw her on the roof."

The breath pushed through his lips so forcefully it was as if he had been punched in the stomach. He stood and stared at me with a look so inexplicable that I instantly wanted to retreat.

"I'm sorry," I whispered, the tears now streaming down my face. "I don't know why I told you that. Don't be mad at Willie."

He stared at me as a tear pushed its way over his lower lid. I watched it slide down his cheek and curl into the corner of his mouth.

"When? When did you see her on the roof?" he asked.

"Weeks ago. It was the first time Willie saw her. I didn't tell you before because I knew it would sound so odd. I don't even know why I'm telling you now. But I had a dream about it, and I thought maybe it would mean something to you."

Michael didn't look well. He appeared afflicted and distraught. I rose from my seat to comfort him, but he backed away from me.

"I need to be alone," he said.

"I'm sorry, Michael. I don't know why . . . I'm just trying to figure this out."

He nodded, but he didn't say anything. The muscles in his neck had tightened, and there was such sorrow in his expression that I was afraid to say anything more. I walked myself to the front door and left him standing in the kitchen, his shoulders slumped from the weight of what I had said, his face wet from the silent tears that he could no longer control.

As I left his house and walked down the front steps, his despair overwhelmed me, and a groan escaped from inside. I covered my mouth and kept walking, trying to hold myself together. The story about the roof had inexplicably escaped from my mouth without any forethought or direction on my part. What was happening to me? Why couldn't I let this go? Why couldn't I get Michael and Jannie out of my head?

I wanted to collapse on the sidewalk and scream at the sky, but I forced my feet to move forward, keenly aware and thankful that my house was only a short distance away. I had to make it inside before I completely lost control. I had to get past the front door before I could let the sobs release from my chest. As a walked down the sidewalk staring at the cracks and errant roots, blinking away the tears, and stifling the groan that threatened to erupt, I tried to take solace in the possibility that there was rational reason for what was happening. I prayed that was true, because if there wasn't a logical explanation for my experiences and questionable behavior, it meant that I was slowly going insane. It meant that I would not just lose Robert, I might lose Willie as well. That would be a loss I could not endure.

Chapter 34

Willie spoke to Robert on the phone that night, but their conversation was brief. I paced the floor as they talked, half listening and half watching the Spains' house through my family room windows. I hadn't seen Michael leave, but his lights were out, and there were no signs of activity. Isabella was quiet too, and I felt very alone.

"Daddy wants to speak with you," Willie said, handing me the phone. I grabbed the receiver, and he immediately left the room, no doubt in a rush to grab one of his comic books and retreat to the world of superheroes that he loved so much.

"We need to talk this through, Charlotte," Robert said, his voice calm but stern.

"I told you my position, Robert. The ball is in your court." I was tired and not sure I had the energy to battle him, but I managed my way through.

"You're being unreasonable," he said, letting his words sit in the air a moment before continuing. "I'll draw up a counterproposal within the next day or two."

"Do what you want, Robert, but I've said my piece. If you aren't willing to do the right thing, then we'll just have to agree to disagree."

"Charlotte, that adultery statute is a joke, and it's never enforced. So if you think you have some leverage here based on some ancient statute that no one gives credence to, you need to rethink that."

It amazed me that he didn't even try to deny his affair, only its legal ramifications. "Listen, Robert. I'm only telling you what my lawyer is telling me. So if you think my demands are a joke, then you'll have to have this discussion with my lawyer."

He was silent for a moment and then asked, "Who's your lawyer?"

The only lawyer I knew was Isabella's lawyer, and I had never spoken to him about handling my divorce. I didn't even know whether he took on such cases. But I was distracted and wanted to get him off the phone, so I blurted out an answer, "His name is Ralph. I'll e-mail you his contact information, but right now I have to go and get Willie settled. Good-bye, Robert."

I hung up the phone before he could press me for any more information. I couldn't talk to him any longer. I felt agitated and uneasy, preoccupied with what had transpired with Michael earlier in the day. What made me go over there? What made me tell him about the roof? Was it simply just the dream, or was it some other force? I couldn't eat. I could barely swallow down the water I forced myself to drink. I didn't feel in control of myself and that worried me beyond belief.

Despite my agitation, I retired early, desperate for the solace that sleep might be able to bring to me, but it was a difficult night. My mind raced with images of Jannie and Michael. I relived my awkward conversation with him over and over again. I was taunted by that look on his face, a look that reflected internal chaos and puzzlement, a look that showed signs of hope but also fear and regret.

Then there was the dream. Snippets of that dream resurfaced each time I started to drift, with Jannie and her son speaking to each other in my head. They spoke of love and the shortness of time. They spoke of living with pain and paining to live. They spoke of hope and destiny. They spoke of a sometimes heartless earth and a windowless heaven.

Not surprisingly, when I did finally fall asleep, it was fitful and restless. I was actually glad to see the morning arrive so I could get out of bed and try to busy myself away from any images and memories of the Spain family. It would eventually prove to be a futile effort.

For that day and the next, I preoccupied myself by cleaning every corner of my house, only leaving when I had to transport Willie from one activity to another. I struggled to keep from looking out my windows, even going so far as to shut my curtains and to rely on artificial light to see my way.

The phone rang more than I can remember it ever ringing. Isabella called frequently, and while I would talk to her, I discouraged her from coming by with tales of feeling ill. I needed separation from the world. I needed to find myself again. I needed to understand who I was without the shadows of Robert and Isabella lurking by my side. But more than anything, I needed to make myself sane so that I would not be tempted to blurt out hurtful observations to Michael or see the images of his dead wife at every turn. I wanted to retreat from the world, but I was trapped by my circumstances. All I could do was retreat into myself, if only for a few short days.

In the late afternoon of the second day, however, the doorbell rang and brought an end to my preoccupation with cleanliness. I was in the middle of scrubbing the master bathroom when I heard the first ring. I ignored it and the second ring as well. By the third ring, I was anxious with the sudden thought that Willie might need me, and I ran down the stairs with the sponge still wet and soapy in my hand. When I opened the door, I didn't recognize the man standing there.

"I'm looking for Charlotte Webb," he said, his face blank of emotion.

"Speaking," I said through the screen door. He looked oddly familiar. There was something in his eyes and the line of his jaw that I recognized.

"I was wondering if I could talk to you." It was not so much a question as a statement. His eyes drifted to the dripping sponge.

"I'm in the middle of something right now. And I really don't have the money to buy anything." I started to close the door.

"You don't understand," he said quickly. "I live next door."

"Next door?" I looked at him more carefully. I hadn't seen him in the neighborhood before, but I had seen him someplace. Then it hit me. I knew his face. I had seen it in the framed photos. "Are you Michael or Paul?"

"Michael," he said.

"All the way from California?"

He nodded and asked, "May I come in for a moment?"

I faltered momentarily, not sure of his intentions. But his face was so like his father's, rimmed with kindness despite the steady core, that I felt compelled to oblige him. "Of course," I said and gestured him through the door. "We can sit on the couch. Let me just throw this in the sink."

I left him sitting on the couch and went into the kitchen. I dropped the sponge into the sink and caught my breath. His presence unnerved me. I hadn't managed to get Michael and Jannie out of my head, but I had somehow suppressed most of the emotions that had been tormenting me. Those feelings would certainly come rushing back the moment he said his mother's name.

I took another deep breath before joining him in the family room. As I entered, I saw in his eyes that he too was afraid. I sat down a safe distance from him and offered a smile. "What did you want to talk about?"

He cleared his throat and sat up straighter. "My father has been talking to Paul . . . my brother. And Paul has been talking to me." He looked at me and waited for a reaction. I didn't give him one. "My Dad and I don't really talk much, but I've been told that you have been talking to him about my mother."

Again, he waited, but I kept my silence. I'm not sure I could have spoken then even if I wanted to. My insides were a mess, and my brain was conflicted on how to best address the situation. I simply sat and met his eyes, my hands clenched tightly on my lap.

"Paul was pretty upset about the things you said to Dad . . . about talking to Mom, about seeing her." He wasn't looking at me now. His head had dropped slightly, and he was nervously playing with his hands, pushing his outstretched fingers in and out of each other like two intermingling webs. He glanced up and continued, "Paul thinks we should keep Dad away."

"Away from what?" I asked.

"Away from you."

"Me? Why?"

"Paul thinks that you are trying to manipulate Dad, work on his emotions for some personal advantage."

"What does he think I would gain from doing that?" I asked, trying to maintain a calm composure. He seemed so trepid, so susceptible at that moment.

He shrugged. "I don't know. Maybe you're lonely. Maybe it's money. We don't really know what's going on, but you need to understand how uncomfortable this is, how suspicious it is for you to make the claims you've made."

I sat on his words for a few moments before responding, "Why are you here, Michael? Did you fly in all the way from California just to tell me to stay away from your father?"

He stared into my eyes, trying to assess me. "I expected you to look different," he said. "I expected you to look a little crazy."

"I may actually be a little crazy, but I have no hidden agenda with your father," I said. "I am as mystified about seeing Jannie . . . your mother . . . as anyone else. It has caused me a great deal of confusion, so I understand your skepticism. I just don't know what to say to you to make you understand. I don't understand it myself."

His shoulders relaxed a bit, and he stopped fumbling with his hands. Then, before he spoke again, he took a slow, cleansing breath. "My brother and I are close, but we are different people. I guess that's probably true of most brothers. When I first heard how you were telling Dad about seeing my mom, I have to admit I was angry, just like Paul. It didn't make any sense to me. My mother didn't even know you. Why wouldn't she come visit me instead?"

"Do you still feel that way?" I asked.

"I heard about the roof, how you saw her on the roof . . . Is that true?"

"Actually, my son saw her there."

"Your son?"

"He's six. He has seen your mother several times too. The first time was on the roof. I didn't believe him when he told me, but your mother told me she had been up there."

"What did she say?" he asked, his voice lowering to a half whisper.

"She could see that it frightened him, that it made him think she was a witch, so she told us she had been up there with the help of some roofing contractors . . . it didn't make much sense frankly, but I didn't know at the time that . . ."

"That what?"

"That she wasn't with us anymore."

"What else did she say to you?"

"We had very brief conversations on the few times I actually spoke to her."

"But what did she say? She must have said something about us, about her family."

"Just how she had left your dad. How troubled he was about it. I thought she meant they had gotten a divorce. I didn't understand at the time. And then we just talked about the roof, about what I already told you."

"That's it? She didn't say anything personal, anything that would make us feel better about all of this?"

"I'm sorry. I wish I had more to tell you. I didn't know she was dead." I stopped and silently cursed myself. "I'm sorry. That sounded harsh. What I mean is that if I had known she had passed, I might have had a different conversation with her. I'm still trying to get over the fact that she talked to me at all!"

His disappointment was evident. "Did she say anything that would confirm that she really spoke to you?"

I thought back to our brief conversations and tried to remember something meaningful, but nothing came to mind. There was nothing in any of our short conversations that struck me as a personal message of any kind. "I can't think of anything. I'm sorry. Maybe I just missed it because I wasn't looking for it."

Michael wanted more from me, and I couldn't give it to him. He started to stand. "Maybe Paul is right. Maybe you need to stay away from my father. At least stop talking to him about my mother. It's not real. If it were real, she would have told you something that we could connect with, something more concrete. I can't imagine my mother would show herself to a complete stranger just for the purpose of a friendly conversation."

He started for the front door. I stood and chased after him. "Wait!"

He turned. "I wanted to believe in you. I had hope even, despite Paul's concerns. But I think I was wrong."

"I am not lying about this, Michael. She said she wanted my help."

"Your help with what?"

"I don't know. I think it has to do with your father. His grief is so deep."

"It should be," he said, then shook his head. "It doesn't matter. Just stay away from him, okay? He really doesn't have that much money anyway."

He opened the door and stepped onto the porch. I felt so desperate, so panicked. I didn't know why exactly, but I couldn't let him leave. I couldn't let him walk away with such low regard for what had happened between Jannie and me, thinking that I was a greedy neighbor with a hidden agenda. Then I remembered the dream, the dream that had stayed with me these past few days, the dream that had enlightened me about the roof.

"Did you have a conversation with your mother on the back porch?" I asked just before he reached the porch steps.

"What are you talking about?" he asked, turning to look at me. There was now a touch of anger in his eyes, but the sadness was even more apparent.

"Before she died, did you speak to her on the back porch? It was a sunny day but a little chilly. She didn't want to go inside." I was rambling, trying to get the story out quickly before he walked away.

"Why are you asking me that?" He was doubtful, but at least I had delayed his departure.

"You wanted her to go inside because it was chilly, but she didn't want to. She liked sitting on the back porch. She liked being outside."

"Lots of people sit on their back porches in the sun," he said, but a glimmer of hope had returned.

"You wanted to take a leave of absence from work, but she told you not to do that, that your father could take care of her."

His lips parted slightly, and he started to blink at a slightly faster pace as if he had experienced a sudden sting in his eyes. He stayed standing at the top of the stairs, one foot still on its way down. "She told you that?"

"In her own way, yes."

He frowned. "Anything else?"

I tried to remember the dream. I tried to remember what she showed me. Was there something more, something he might connect with? When I hesitated, he started to turn. I stepped toward him.

"You wanted a sign from her."

"Everyone wants a sign," he said and started down the steps.

"She said she would find a way to show you she was okay."

"Everyone wants that too." He stepped onto the sidewalk.

"Your father teased her about the roof, about how she always wanted to go up there and see the view."

"He could have told you that," he said, continuing down the walk. "I hadn't thought of that before, but he could have told you. Maybe he just doesn't remember mentioning it."

"No, he has never spoken to me of Jannie. He doesn't like to talk about her with me." My eyes began to fill up. My heart was thumping, thumping in my chest. Then it came to me, and I yelled for to him to stop.

"Wait," I said, hurrying down the steps. "She loves the view."

He stopped instantly, but he didn't immediately turn around. He waited to see if I had more to say.

I stopped myself on the sidewalk, a mere ten feet from where he now stood with his back to me. His breathing had deepened, and his back moved with each breath.

"She's at peace, Michael," I said. "Your mother doesn't need to look through any windows to see the beauty of the world. There are no windows in heaven."

His back began to shake, and I realized that he had begun to cry. I walked down the sidewalk until I reached him. He turned and looked at me, his face now wet. He reached forward and hugged me, his tears now flowing freely. Between sobs, he managed to whisper, "I was hoping you'd say that. Oh god, I was hoping you'd say that."

Chapter 35

"You need to forgive him," I said as I refilled his mug of coffee. After the experience earlier, neither one of us wanted to part ways too quickly. So Michael Jr. had joined me inside for a few cups of coffee and a long chat. I told him of my experiences with his mother in more detail. I even bared my soul and confessed to my encounter with Jannie inside his father's house, including the part where I broke in through the back door. Surprisingly, he was not angry at my destructive intrusion. Instead, he found it humorous that his mother had hounded me to such a point of desperation.

Unlike his brother, Paul, Michael was generally trusting of people and very spiritual. Perhaps that's why he took it so hard when he felt betrayed or let down. My experiences with his mother and my conveyance of that important message meant he now trusted me, even after I confessed to breaking into his childhood home. His trust was an honor I took very seriously.

"Maybe she wanted you to go in there so you would see our photos," he had said to me. "So that you would recognize me when I showed up at your door."

"Maybe," I had responded, but I wasn't sure. After all, I had not recognized him right away despite the photos.

"Either way, she seems to have accomplished what she wanted, to get me to come here so you could convey her message," he had said, smiling brightly. What had once been so overwhelming that it nearly brought him to his knees on the sidewalk was now a source of peace and relief.

Having fully discussed my experiences with his mother, we were now talking about his father, a subject that still brought him stress. "I'm just so angry," he said. "I don't understand how he could let that happen to her.

He was supposed to be taking care of her. She trusted him." He blew over the top of the mug to cool the coffee and then sipped at the edge.

"How old are you, Michael?"

"Twenty-four."

"You are so young, too young to have such anger. I'm sure your mother wouldn't want you to blame him. She has found a way to let you know that she's at peace. It's time you found some peace as well."

He nodded, seeming to understand. "Why do you think she came to you?" he asked. It wasn't a question filled with accusation or anger, but genuine curiosity.

"I'm not sure. It's not like I'm prone to these experiences. I have never seen a ghost before or had anything near what I would call a psychic experience. Maybe I have and just didn't know it. But one thing has struck me as odd, a connection I have with your mother that may have made it easier for her to communicate with me somehow."

He furrowed his brow. "What connection?"

"Our birthday. We were both born on March thirtieth."

"Really? That's interesting. Who knows. Maybe birthdays open a window of sorts."

"Maybe. Maybe your mother is looking through a window after all, just long enough to say hello."

He smiled and said, "She would want me to forgive him. I know that. But how do I get myself to do that? It's not as easy as it sounds. I've tried, but I can't get past the anger."

"There's no secret to it. Just do it. Tell him you forgive him. Over time, your brain and your heart will fully accept it."

He nodded. "It was easier for Paul. He placed his blame on the doctor. Not that I didn't, but I blamed Dad too, because Mom was so trusting of him . . ." His voice trailed off. "She didn't let me move here to help her because he was going to take care of her."

"Your father loved your mother very deeply. Trust me, he is blaming himself every day for what happened. I see it in his face. I hear it in his words. When we go to doctors, we trust that they know what they're doing and that they're sober when they're treating us. Based on the newspaper articles I read and what his wife has told me, Dr. Capello was very well respected in his field. He was a very good doctor until the alcohol impaired him. There's no way your father could have known—"

"His wife? You know Capello's wife?"

His question caught me off guard. I hadn't realized that he had not been told that part of the story, how Isabella Capello was now living two doors down from his family home. Apparently, Michael Sr. had not conveyed that detail to his sons.

"Yes, she lives on the other side of me." I felt compelled to tell him, to honor his trust in me.

"What? How did that happen?"

"She doesn't own the house. The owner is letting her stay there until she gets through some legal issues."

"Legal issues?"

"You know that Dr. Capello died earlier this year, don't you?"

"That part I knew. Paul told me about it. I guess I also knew that his widow was a suspect, but I live so far away that I haven't really kept tabs on it. Far as I'm concerned, he's where he should be, and I doubt it's in the same place as my mother." He stood up and arched his neck as he looked out the back window. "This house over here," he said, pointing in the direction of Isabella's backyard. "She lives right there?"

"Yes. She's actually very nice, Michael."

"So she's still a suspect, huh?"

"Actually, they just charged her with murder."

He turned and tilted his head to the side. "Did she do it? Did she set the fire?"

"No. She didn't do it."

"How do you know?"

I told him some of the details of the expert report, but I didn't tell him her side of the story. That was Isabella's tale to tell, not mine.

"Maybe that fire was just karma kicking that drunken doctor in the ass." He stood by the window, still gazing over at Isabella's home.

"Maybe. Or maybe it was just a tragic accident."

He turned to me, a flash of anger in his eyes. "He murdered my mother. That fire was no accident."

Chapter 36

I stood on the porch and hugged Michael good-bye. He kissed my cheek and headed back to his father's house. He had barely made it to the sidewalk when Isabella strode up, a smirk on her face.

"I thought you were sick," she said.

"I'm feeling much better."

"He's cute," she said, batting her lashes. "A little young, but that's okay."

"That was Michael Spain *Jr.*," I said, and her eyes immediately lifted.

"Really? How come you're so cozy with *him*?"

"Because he actually believes that I have spoken to his mother."

Isabella walked up the porch steps, flashing me one of her classic looks, a look that at once expressed friendship as well as doubt. She was, as always, dressed impeccably.

"I just got back from my lawyer's office," she said, choosing not to engage in a spiritual discussion. "The prosecutor has refused to drop the charges."

"What? Did he read your expert's report?"

"Oh yes, but he remains convinced of my guilt for reasons far too numerous for me to repeat."

"So what does that mean?" I asked, my nerves suddenly awake again.

Isabella reached the top step and leaned against the porch post. "It means I'll have to go through a trial. Probably before the end of the year if things keep going at the pace they're going."

"I'm sorry. I really thought that report would set you free."

Isabella shrugged. "So why was Junior over here anyway?"

I sighed and returned the look she had given me earlier. I was hesitant to share my experience with her because I knew she would not trust in it. "Let's just say he's my new friend and leave it at that."

Isabella shook her head and smiled. "Okay, Charlotte. I'll let you keep your secrets, at least for a little while."

"Do you want to come in?" I asked. "I can make us something to eat."

"That sounds wonderful. I'm starving."

Isabella joined me in the kitchen, and together we whipped up a batch of pasta. I set the table and put out the shredded parmesan and a cup of capers. "Should we have some wine?" I asked.

"That's becoming a habit with us, isn't it?" Isabella said.

"We could have something else if you want."

She looked at me curiously, and then we both started to laugh. I grabbed a bottle of Cabernet from the cabinet and set it on the table with two goblets. I was just starting to make our plates when Willie came through the back door.

"Hi, sweetie," I said. "Did you have fun at Ben's house?"

"It was okay," he said, looking tired.

"Are you hungry? Want some pasta?"

"Okay," he said, sitting down next to Isabella. She reached over and ruffled his hair, which eased a smile out of his frown.

"Why so sad?" she asked him.

Willie shrugged and started to flip the spoon in the container of shredded cheese.

"Willie, don't do that," I said, putting a small plate of pasta in front of him. "What happened at Ben's?"

"Nothin'," he said and then instantly offered a slight explanation. "His parents are getting a divorce."

Isabella and I shared a look before I asked, "How do you know that?"

"Ben told me. He said he didn't care, but I could tell that he did. Are you and Dad getting a divorce too?"

Willie looked up at me with his big brown eyes. His face was tanned from many days spent in the summer sun, and there was a line of sweat where his forehead met his hairline. I didn't have the heart to tell him the truth. I also didn't have the heart to lie to him. "It's a possibility, Willie. Your father and I have to talk and figure out what's best for everyone."

Willie didn't say anything. He poked his fork into the pasta and slowly turned the strings of spaghetti around the metal prongs. He didn't eat, content for now to simply twirl and stare at his plate.

It was a quiet dinner. Isabella did her best to engage Willie in discussion, but he had few words to offer. He eventually finished his meal and asked to be excused. I let him leave the table and listened as he plodded through the front rooms and up the wooden stairway.

"He seemed really tired," Isabella said, still sipping at her first glass of wine.

"And sad," I whispered.

"He'll be okay, Charlotte, just like you said."

"I've been known to be wrong sometimes."

She smiled. "That's true. But not when it comes to Willie."

Isabella stood up and cleared our plates from the table. She instantly started washing them in the sink.

"Don't do that," I said. "I'll get to it later."

"You sit down," she commanded, waving a soapy dish at me. "You deserve to be helped out once in a while."

"At least let me dry," I said and stood next to her at the sink, a dishtowel now in my hand.

"Have you heard from Robbie?" she asked as she rinsed off a dish and handed it to me.

"I talked to him a few days ago. I told him Ralph was my lawyer and that I would send him his information." I grabbed the last glass from her hands and started to dry it. Isabella started to rinse the soap from the sink.

"My Ralph? Really? I didn't know he handled divorces."

"I haven't actually talked to him yet, so I have no idea if he can help me."

Isabella turned off the water and leaned against the sink, her hand now arched firmly on her hip. "What are you waiting for, Charlotte? You need to get a lawyer before Robbie takes all of your money and this house too. Let's call Ralph right now."

Isabella started toward the phone and began to dial. I reached over and hit the receiver. She looked at me bewildered.

"I have no money for a lawyer."

"Neither did I, but I got Ralph because he agreed to take a third of my insurance money as his payment if he wins the case for me."

"Really?"

"Sure. If he gets me off the criminal charges, the insurance company's going to have a tough time fighting my insurance claim. We're talking a huge payout for the both of us." Isabella turned back to the sink. She sprayed the remaining soap and dirty grime down the drain until the sink was clean. Then she turned to me again. "I'll talk to Ralph for you. If he can't handle your case, maybe he'll know someone who can. Just don't let Robbie know you don't have a lawyer yet."

Her words of a big payout rang in my ears, but I didn't have much time to think about it before the back door opened and caught my attention.

"Do you *live* here now?" Robert asked as he walked into the house.

"You really should knock before entering," Isabella scoffed.

"This is still my house, sweetie," he said and turned his attention to me.

"I've been calling you for the past two days. Why aren't you answering the phone? And how come the answering machine is turned off?"

Isabella smiled and winked at me, but she said nothing.

"I haven't been feeling well," I lied. "So I turned off the ringer and the recorder."

"You look fine now," he said, shooting an evil look at Isabella. She didn't so much as flinch. "So turn them back on. I need you and William to be reachable."

I could see the words forming in Isabella's mouth, so I spoke quickly before she had a chance to say something. "I'll turn the ringer back on, but I'll have to think about the answering machine."

Robert glared at Isabella. "You need to leave," he demanded. "Charlotte and I need to speak in private."

"I don't think so," she said sweetly. "I haven't finished my wine."

Isabella walked over to the kitchen table and sat down. She reached for her wineglass and started to lift it to her lips. Robert's eyes flashed, and the vein on the side of his head started to pulsate.

"I want her out of here, Charlotte."

"Well, I don't," I said, sitting at the table next to Isabella. "She's my friend, and we are in the middle of a conversation. You can't just barge in here and make demands."

"You two are always in the middle of a conversation," he yelled, his hands now clenching his hips. He raised his arm and pointed at Isabella, but his eyes remained on me. "She's a murderer, and she shouldn't be in this house when my son's around."

Isabella slid back her chair with a quick push. Her wineglass tipped and sprayed red liquid across the wooden table. As I reached for the glass, I heard his voice behind me.

"Who's a murderer? Isabella?"

The three of us turned to see Willie standing in the doorway.

"Who did she kill?" he asked, looking puzzled and a bit scared.

"No one, Willie," I said, approaching him and guiding him back through the doorway to the family room. "You shouldn't listen in on adult conversations. You misunderstood what we were talking about."

"But Daddy said—"

"No, he didn't. He was talking about something else," I stuttered. "Now go upstairs and get ready for bed."

"It's too early," he complained.

"I don't care. We need to have an adult conversation, so you need to go upstairs. After you wash up and brush your teeth, you can watch television in my room while we finish up down here."

I walked Willie to the stairs and up a few steps. Then I waited as he made the rest of the trek to the top floor and slammed his bedroom door shut. I could hear Isabella and Robert going at it before I even made it back to the family room.

"You're going to rot in jail when this is through," Robert screamed at her.

"Even if that's true, I'm still going to enjoy watching you get what's coming to you," Isabella said, but she was not yelling. She had already cleaned up the wine and had refilled her glass. She was standing now and spoke calmly, her voice absent of any emotional lilt. She seemed to enjoy Robert's inability to maintain the same composure.

"What are you talking about?" Robert stammered, his voice still loud and angry. "That ridiculous adultery statute?"

"Well, that too," she said. "But no, I was thinking of something a little more threatening to that legal career of yours."

Robert blinked, perhaps a bit too much, before balking. "You're so full of shit."

"That's enough," I interjected. "You need to leave, Robert."

"But we were having so much fun," Isabella said, her words still soft and melodic.

"What the hell are you up to?" Robert asked, nearing Isabella. I quickly stood between them.

"You need to leave," I said, raising my voice just enough to get Robert's attention.

"I'm not going anywhere until she tells me what the hell she's talking about."

"Sounds like you have something to worry about, Robbie. Maybe now you'll stop making things so difficult for Charlotte and agree to what she's asked you."

"Isabella, please. This isn't helping," I said, still standing between them. "Please, Robert, just leave."

"I'm not leaving until she is out of this house," Robert commanded. He was speaking with such force that I felt a spray of his spit hit my cheek. "What the hell is going on between the two of you anyway?"

"Why? Is that a fantasy of yours?" Isabella asked.

"Trust me, you aren't in any of my fantasies."

Isabella cocked her head and flashed her white teeth at him. "Thank God," she hissed and then sipped at her wine.

Robert stared at her in an effort to make her uncomfortable, using the same, condescending look he often gave me. But Isabella did not shy away. With each sip of wine, her eyes remained on his, one eyebrow slightly arched as if to challenge him.

Robert slowly let his steely gaze shift to me. "You're forcing my hand, Charlotte," he said. "If I need to get William out of this house to keep him away from this killer, I will."

Isabella still did not flinch, but I could now see the hate festering behind her brown eyes. Before I could speak, she warned him, "If you even try to take Willie away, Robbie, all bets are off."

Robert's eyes blackened. "You don't have anything on me, Isabella."

"I know more than I care to," she said, her eyes still fixed upon his. She swirled the wine in her mouth, swallowed slowly, and then puckered her lips ever so slightly.

Robert was not amused. He turned to me again. "I mean it, Charlotte. You have about three seconds to make her leave, or I'm taking William out of this house."

"You're not touching my son," I said.

Isabella stepped forward. "Do they allow young boys to stay in that hotel of yours?" she asked, setting her glass down on the kitchen table.

Robert started for the front room. "I'm getting my son out of here."

Isabella turned as he walked past her and said, "Where will he sleep, Robbie? Does room 104 actually have two beds?"

Robert stopped and turned around slowly. His face was now twisted with anger, and his body had tensed. The veins on the side of his neck throbbed, like the fleshy throat of a toad. In an instant, he started forward with his right arm raised as if he was going to take a swipe at Isabella. I jumped between them and reached my own arm up in protection. Robert knocked against me, causing me to stumble backward into her. We both nearly fell under the force of his weight.

"What is wrong with you!" I screamed, pushing him away with both hands.

"I want her out of this house! I want that fucking bitch out of this house!" He thrust his finger at her like he was picking out a criminal in a police lineup.

"What is she talking about, Robert? What hotel?" I asked.

Robert grabbed hold of my arms and forced me to look at him. "Charlotte," he said, his words spewing with hatred. "She's been charged with murdering her husband, for Christ's sake! She's here only because someone was dumb enough to pay her bail. Why would you listen to anything she has to say? Why are you exposing yourself and our son to the likes of her?"

"Let her go, Robbie," Isabella said, pulling my right arm from his grip. It was the first time she had raised her voice.

"Shut up, bitch!" he yelled at her as I pulled my other arm free.

"Stop! Both of you!" I begged.

"Why don't you tell her, Robbie? It's going to come out eventually."

Robert's face was marred by sweat now, and the veins on his temple and neck throbbed with such force that they looked ready to explode. His hair was messed, and sweat stains started to show through his pressed shirt.

"How you killed your husband, Isabella? How you got him so drunk that he passed out? How you planted a few pieces of evidence around him to make it look like he tried to put out a fire, and then you doused him and that damn couch with liquor before lighting up a cigar and throwing it and a bunch of newspapers into your homemade stew!"

"I've already heard this new theory," Isabella said with a tilt of her head and a shrug of her shoulders.

"It's no theory. We know exactly how this happened. I just want to know how long you stayed around before leaving. Did you wait for him to die? Did you watch the fire tear through his clothes and burn some of the skin off his legs?"

I glanced at Isabella and saw her mouth twitch. With a cold stare, she met Robert's glare and said, "I did not kill my husband, and you know it."

"Yes, you did, Mrs. Capello. You most certainly did. That stupid report of yours by that gun-for-hire isn't changing anyone's mind. He must be getting paid a lot of money by that shit lawyer of yours. What's his name? Ralph?" He turned to me and started to laugh. "Is that who you've retained as your lawyer? Oh shit, doesn't that make sense. That's perfect, just perfect!" Robert threw back his head and laughed even louder as if he finally understood a good joke. Then he looked at Isabella with disdain. "You must be promising him a shitload of money to handle your defense . . . or maybe you're paying him in an even better way."

"Fuck you," she whispered.

"No, thanks. I prefer money for my services."

Isabella's face iced over, but instead of speaking to Robert, she spoke to me. "Do you want to know who your husband's been shacking up with?" she asked, lifting her glass from the table and swallowing down the rest of the wine. When I didn't answer her, she said, "I believe her name is Laura."

"Shut your fucking mouth!" Robert cursed, taking a step forward.

"She's a pretty girl, well dressed and clean," Isabella continued, now turning to Robert, her ruby-red lips turning into a broad smirk. "But young, barely old enough to legally drink the champagne you had in your hand the other night."

Robert's chin lifted, and his head tilted slightly to the right. With a clenched jaw, he forced out his next words, "You fucking bitch."

"The funny thing is," she continued, "my sources tell me she's still married too, to another lawyer in fact. I think he works for you at the firm, doesn't he? Laura did seem a bit too young to be married to a partner. Plus, that would be a bit risky even for you."

Robert kept his eyes upon her, like a cougar watching his prey. I began to panic when I saw that predatory look in his eyes. Isabella, however, did not let up. "Does Laura's husband know you're fucking his wife? That could be an awfully tough thing to explain, especially with you being his boss and all."

Robert looked like he was about to spit on her, and I suddenly felt nauseous. "Is that true, Robert?" I asked.

Robert glared at Isabella a moment longer and then turned to me, that old look of disdain and disrespect in his face. "You're going to believe this murdering bitch?"

"She's my friend, and I trust her."

"You were never very smart, Charlotte, but you can't be *that* stupid!"

My hand reacted before my mind gave thought to it, and I slapped him so quickly and with such force that I could see the red print of my palm and fingers on his cheek almost instantly. Robert took a step back and hesitated.

Isabella instinctively moved forward, reached out her hand, and pulled me behind her. She kept her eyes on Robert and waited. There were a few short moments of awkward silence before we heard the Spains' screen door slam open and the pounding of footsteps across the backyard. Robert stomped up to Isabella and grabbed her upper arms. He whispered, "We'll finish this later," and then he quickly turned for the front door.

Chapter 37

Michael and his son dashed through the screen door just as Robert was leaving through the front.

"Are you okay?" Michael asked, sweat shining on his forehead. Junior stood close behind, a curious but worried look on his face.

Isabella waited for me to answer, but I couldn't speak through the anger welling inside.

"Well?" Michael persisted. "Is everything all right? It looked like things were getting a bit physical."

"Robbie just wanted me to leave," Isabella said, glancing in my direction. When I still didn't say anything, she continued, "He doesn't like me hanging around Charlotte. He thinks I'm a bad influence."

Junior made his way next to his father and gave Isabella the once-over. "Are you the doctor's wife?" he asked.

She cocked her head and lifted her left brow. "My name's Isabella."

"Charlotte, what's going on?" Michael asked, his arms outstretched as if he wanted to physically pull an explanation out of me.

I pulled out the kitchen chair and sat down. "Robert was threatening to take Willie," I said.

"What? Why?"

"Because of me," Isabella said, offering an apologetic look.

"Have you been following him?" I asked her, the anger resurfacing. "Have you been spying on Robert?"

Isabella sat down across from me. "I was just trying to help you," she said. "I figured you'd need something on him if you were going to get anything out of this divorce."

"What divorce?" Michael asked. He and his son were both staring at me now, and I noticed for the first time just how much they looked alike.

They had the same jawline and the same tall forehead. Even their eyes were mirror images.

"Robert wants a divorce," I said. "And Isabella decided to take it upon herself to act as my private investigator."

"Why are you so angry at me?" she asked. "Isn't Robbie the bad guy in all of this?"

"I already know he's cheating on me, Isabella. Why did you have to embarrass me by telling me the details? You think it's helpful to tell me my husband's sleeping with a young married woman? How the hell do you even know that?"

Michael and his son were silent, but they didn't leave. Like me, they waited for her answer.

"I didn't mean to hurt you. I wasn't going to say anything to you for that very reason. I was going to wait and see if it became necessary. But he kept pushing me and threatening to take Willie."

"But is it true?"

She was hesitant now, a trait I didn't often see in her. "I've been following him recently. I have a lot of time on my hands, you know." She smiled faintly, but I didn't feel inclined to offer one back. "One night I saw him meet this girl at a hotel. She seemed really young, so I waited around until she left. Then I followed her home and figured out who she was."

"Just like that?"

"It didn't take much to put it all together. I knew he had to be sleeping with someone from work. I just didn't expect it would be another lawyer's wife."

It was then that I realized that I was actually angrier with myself than with her. Isabella didn't sit around and let the Roberts of the world dictate her direction. She saw things for what they were. She grasped the reality of a problem and dealt with it head-on. I, on the other hand, let myself slowly die in the ignorance of my own situation. I had allowed Robert to manipulate and mistreat me. But worse than that, I had blamed myself for his behavior, so much so that the truth of what he was doing and who he was doing it with had become irrelevant. By making myself the bad guy, by allowing myself to believe that I had forced him into someone else's bed, I had allowed the details of his betrayal to lose any significance. Isabella had not fallen into the same trap, and by doing what I should have done, she forced me to recognize my own weakness, my own failures. At that moment, I both admired and hated her.

But my conflicting emotions had another source as well. Isabella was simply too good at being secretive and manipulative. She was too adept at deciphering and addressing a bad situation. Those old feelings of doubt resurfaced in my head.

"I don't know what to think about you," I whispered.

"What do you mean?" she asked.

"Sometimes you scare me."

"Why, Charlotte?" she asked. When I didn't answer her, she asked the same question that I was already asking myself, "Do you still think I killed Anthony? I thought we were past that."

"Didn't you kill him?" Junior chimed in. I had forgotten he was there.

"Michael!" his father scolded.

"What? I don't care if she killed him. I just want to know."

Isabella turned to him, squinting her eyes in an effort to keep her emotions in check. The tiny wrinkles in her forehead were now showing through her makeup. "Anthony did a horrible thing when he failed your mother," she said, her voice cracking slightly. "But he was a good doctor once, a great doctor actually. And despite all of his failures, I still loved him."

"There's a fine line between love and hate," Junior said, keeping his eyes upon her.

"That's true, but there's a pretty thick line between wanting to hurt someone and actually doing it." Isabella turned back to me. "I don't know what else I can say to you, Charlotte. I have tried to be your friend. I have told you more about my life, about that night, than anyone else besides my lawyer." She began to tear up. "I was simply trying to help you."

"But you do things that other people only imagine doing. You always take that extra step."

"And you think that makes me capable of murder?"

"I didn't say that. I just think . . . sometimes you do things without any thought of the costs." I just wanted her to leave. I wanted them all to leave. I wanted to go to bed and hide from the world. I wanted to forget about Robert and Isabella and all of the ugly things that surrounded them.

"That doctor killed my mother, Charlotte. He deserved to die. Frankly, I hope she did kill him."

Michael turned to his son. "Stop it! You need to stay out of this."

"No, I don't. I was pulled into this the day that bastard poisoned Mom."

"Charlotte, maybe we should all leave," Michael said. "You've been through enough tonight."

"I want to know what happened," Junior said, looking at Isabella. "I need to know."

"That's enough. We're leaving," Michael said, grabbing hold of his son's arm and pulling him toward the door.

Junior wrestled his arm free and stepped toward Isabella. "I need to know if you killed that bastard."

"Why are you doing this?" Michael asked. "Why does it matter? They're both dead. End of story!"

"It's not that simple for me, Dad! She was my mother. I need closure. I need to know who brought him down. Was it God? Or was it this woman right here?"

"Knowing who decided his fate isn't going to bring your mother back!" Michael scolded, his anger evident.

"No, but it will sure as hell help me sleep better at night."

Isabella ignored their ranting. She was only interested in me. I felt her searching my face. I desperately wanted to give her the understanding and support she needed, but something was holding me back.

"Charlotte, I need to know once and for all if you believe me," she said, her voice barely above a whisper. "I can't keep doing this with you. There's only so much a person can take before—"

"Before they crack?" Junior asked, avoiding his father's glare.

"Before they realize they are truly alone," she said, talking more to herself than anyone else in the room.

"You're not alone," Michael offered suddenly. He took a deep breath and then started to rub his forehead with his right hand. His fingers were shaking.

"What do you mean, Dad?" Junior asked.

"You just need to leave her be. She didn't kill him," he said, his eyes now closed. His hand was still upon his forehead, aggressively massaging the skin from the sides toward the center with his thumb and fingers. He squinted as if suffering from a headache.

Isabella seemed as stunned as I was, but she said nothing. She was looking at Michael curiously. My eyes switched from Michael to her and back again. Michael took a deep breath and dropped his head, leaving his hands to rest on his hips.

"Michael," I said, standing. "Are you okay?"

"We should go," he said, but he didn't look at any of us.

"Dad, what's going on? Do you know something?"

"Michael?" I asked, approaching him and lifting his head with my hand. His eyes were red and glossy, and the skin on his cheeks was drawn down as if pulled by a gravitational force. I put my palm on the side of his face, and he willingly accepted it, leaning his head so that I felt the weight of his jaw in my palm.

"You should believe her," he said, raising up his arm and placing his hand against my own. "Just believe her."

"Why are you saying that?" Junior asked.

Michael raised his head now, taking hold of my hand as he did. His palm was warm and sweaty, but it felt comfortable against my own skin. Then, with sadness and regret, he looked at his eldest son and said, "Because I was there."

Chapter 38

An awkward silence hung in the air of my kitchen as we registered what Michael had just said. He was still holding my hand, gripping it really, and there was a line of sweat trickling down the side of his face.

Junior was stricken, his face suddenly ashen. I could now see his chest pushing in and out with each deep breath he took. He stood there, stunned into silence, gaping at his father.

Even Isabella seemed at a loss for words, but what she had to say next took me completely by surprise. "You don't have to do this," she whispered.

"Do what?" I asked. "What's going on?"

I looked at Isabella and saw that she had captured Michael's attention. She was shaking her head, signaling him to stop. There was a definite connection between them that I had somehow missed before. I could see it now though in the way they looked at each other.

"I have to do something," Michael said. "Enough's enough."

"Dad, maybe we should talk about this at home," Junior said, with much less energy and force than he had displayed earlier. That worried look had returned, and his fingers started to fidget with the bottom of his shirt.

"You said you needed to know what happened that night, son. And now I'm going to tell you."

"Michael, stop. This isn't necessary." Isabella was rising as she spoke, her eyes intent upon him.

"What's going on?" I asked, wondering even as the words came out whether I really wanted to know the answer to my own question.

"Charlotte, there's something we haven't told you, something I need to say to all of you."

"Please, Michael," Isabella interjected. "We already talked about this. You don't need to get involved."

"I'm already involved," he said, releasing my hand.

I felt my breath catch and instinctively took a step backward. I bumped into Junior, who was standing behind me, and felt his hands grab hold of my upper arms. He didn't immediately let go. "I don't understand," I said. "I thought you didn't know each other until that night Robert got hurt."

"We didn't know each other," Isabella said, avoiding my eyes.

"Charlotte, it's complicated," Michael said, stumbling for the words to tell what he knew.

"I don't know if I want to hear this," Junior interjected. He was still holding on to my arms, keeping me in the space between him and his father. It was as if he was using me as a shield to protect him from whatever was about to come in his direction.

"Well I want to know what the hell's going on," I said. "You two obviously know more about each other than you've let on."

Isabella started to speak, but Michael silenced her. "Let me explain this, Isabella," he said. "You've been kind enough to keep me out of this, but I need to handle it from here."

"Are you sure, Michael?" she asked. "Once a word is spoken, it can't be silenced again."

He nodded and gestured me and Junior to the table. "You might want to sit for this."

We both moved to the open chairs and sat down as instructed. Isabella sat back down as well. None of us said anything, but I'm certain Junior felt the same sickness that I felt creeping into my gut. I was so fearful of what Michael might say that I actually pulled my hand to my mouth to cover up the painful sounds I feared would release from my throat when his truth revealed itself.

"When Jannie died, I blamed myself," Michael said, standing near where we all sat. "But I blamed the doctor more. I felt such anger, such hatred towards him. I had never felt like that before, not in my entire life. I started fantasizing about killing him. I wanted him to die for killing my dear Jannie. At first, it was a thought that popped into my head maybe a few times a day. But as the weeks passed and turned into months, it slowly became an obsession. I found myself constantly thinking about Dr. Capello and how I might kill him. My sadness, the pain of losing her, was so unbearable." He choked back the sorrow that had resurfaced. "I was so stricken I wanted to die. But I knew that would destroy my sons. I couldn't leave them too." He looked at Junior, whose own face now reflected the grief his father spoke of.

Michael continued, "I convinced myself that I could not survive, that I could not escape from that dark hole I was in unless I punished Dr. Capello for what he did to my wife." He rubbed his palm down the side of his face, smearing the sweat that still sparkled on his skin. "So I took that extra step you just talked about, Charlotte. At first, I just drove by his house and thought about what I would do. Would I get a gun? A knife? Would I just beat the hell out of him? All these thoughts raced through my mind. It was constant. I couldn't think of anything else . . . anything else besides that damn doctor and my dear Jannie. I must have driven by his house half a dozen times. A few times I even stopped and stared at his neatly manicured lawn and draped windows, wondering if he was enjoying the happiness he had stolen from me."

Michael walked to the back window and stared into the yard. It was getting dark now, and there was a crack of thunder in the distance. He continued, "I wanted him to die slowly, just like she did. I wanted him to know it was coming. Not for a second or a minute, but for as long as possible . . ."

He inhaled the air through his nose, and released it roughly from the back of his throat. "One night I had a few drinks, and the thoughts became stronger, clearer in my head. What I had been obsessing about for so long suddenly became urgent. It was as if I couldn't live another day without doing something, without releasing all of that anger and hate, without acting on what I had thought about day and night for so many weeks . . ."

Michael walked toward the side window and looked out at his house across the way. "Jannie and I had been happy, so happy together for all of those years. We had the perfect life. He stole that from me. He took away the mother of my sons. He denied her the joy of being a grandmother." His back started to tremble, and an odd sound released from deep inside his body. It was the sorrowful groan of a man who had lost part of his soul. Junior started to stand, but I grabbed hold of his arm and shook my head. He reluctantly sat back down, his own tears now streaking down his face.

I looked at Isabella. She was sitting with her head in her hands, her eyes closed behind a web of fingers. Her breathing was fast and deep. I knew then how difficult this was for her. I reached my hand over and grabbed hold of her arm, pulling her hand from her face until I could cup it in my own. She opened her eyes momentarily and graced me with a gentle but quickly fading smile. I gripped her hand and was relieved when she returned the squeeze.

Another sob erupted from Michael's mouth, and in his effort to swallow it back, he began to choke. Again, Junior started to rise. Again, I tried to hold him back, but I could not keep him in his chair. He gave his father some distance, but he stood now, ready to go to his father's aid if it came to that.

Michael ran his hand across his eyes and quickly wiped away the moisture from his nose and mouth. Then he continued, "I drove over there that night and parked my car down the street. I walked to the front door. I was going to confront him before I took his life. I was about to knock when I heard their voices. I heard screaming and shouting from inside." He turned and faced Isabella, his face still wet and swollen, but she did not look up. "So I walked around to the backyard and looked through the windows. They were open, and I could hear everything. I saw Isabella there . . . I saw her slap him. I saw his drink fly out of his hand. Then I saw him hit her . . ."

Isabella started to weep. Her head was now cradled in one hand, but I kept my grip on the other. She fought to drown out the sounds that made their way from deep inside, but it was a fight she could not win.

"I saw Isabella leave," he continued. "That was my chance, my turn to make him pay for what he had done to my family." Michael looked at his son briefly and then turned to the windows again. He took another deep breath, his body visibly trembling now. "I had a gun with me. It had been my father's. I had never used it before Jannie died, had never even taken it out of the storage box in the attic. I had to drive to a shooting range two hours away just to make sure it still worked . . . Anyway, I stood outside the window and watched him after Isabella left, that gun tight in my hand. I stood there for a long time trying to muster the courage to go inside, watching as he spoke to someone on the phone and poured himself another drink. He was a wreck, stumbling all over the place. I had hate and fury in my heart, but I couldn't get past the windows. I knew that once I went inside, my life would forever change. I would no longer be the person I had been . . ."

He turned back to us, his face still wet from the emotions that continued to release, his shoulders low as if someone was pulling his arms to the floor. He looked at Junior and shook his head in disbelief. "Then I saw the fire start. That fool was drunk, stumbling around with a lighter and cigar, spilling his drink all over the place. He eventually dropped his cigar on the couch . . . at first it was just a small flame. He even tried to pat it out with his bare hands. When that didn't work, he tried to smother it with the newspaper, which was still wet with whatever liquor he was drinking. That only made things worse. He never did put the drink down, kept it in his hand as he smacked the newspaper against the couch. I stood outside that window, the gun in my hand, and I watched as that fire got bigger and bigger . . . it rose so quickly. The flames were so bright, with an orange and yellow glow that flickered against the glass of the windows.

I realized then that the fire would take him before I got my revenge, before I could release the despair that was tormenting me, before I could pay him back for what he did to Jannie. So I finally went inside. I finally found the courage to do what I came to do. I didn't make it more than ten steps through the door when I started to feel the effects of the poison in the air. It was awful. The smoke. The smell. I couldn't breathe. I ran back out and stood in the grass again, looking through that damn window, watching the doctor die from the fire he had started, angry that I was being denied the right to . . ."

Michael stopped himself and turned to Isabella. She was looking up now, her own face a mess of wetness and failing makeup. Michael continued, "When Isabella returned, I was at the back corner of the house, the gun still in my hand. I was near a stand of trees, afraid to move for fear she would hear my shoes on the grass. There were twigs and pinecones all over the lawn. So I stayed where I was and prayed she wouldn't see me in the darkness. But I underestimated the power of the fire and the light it cast through the windows. The fire had grown and spread so fast. At first, she stood by the picture window and looked inside, just like I had done. But then she unexpectedly turned toward me. Her eyes locked on the gun. Then she looked up at me. I panicked and ran. I never looked back."

Michael wiped his eyes with the short sleeve of his shirt and exhaled. "I read the story in the paper the next day. It was all over the news. When I read later that she was a suspect, that they thought she killed her husband, I thought about coming forward, about telling my story. But I was scared . . . I had gone to that house with a loaded, unregistered gun, with every intent to kill that doctor." He shook his head, his eyes glazed over in the memory. "I don't know if I could have actually done it, but that was my intent. How would I be able to explain my presence there? He had been my wife's doctor . . . there was a malpractice charge pending against him for her death . . . Isabella had seen me with the gun . . . I didn't know what to do. So I decided to wait and see . . . I decided to wait and hope that my involvement wouldn't become necessary . . ."

Michael turned again to Isabella. "I'm sorry I didn't come forward all those months ago. I'm so sorry for what you've been through."

Isabella met his gaze. She nodded but still said nothing. She was still weeping, too tired and beaten to speak any further.

"I don't understand," I said, my own voice sounding foreign to my ears. "When did you tell Isabella that it was you she saw that night?"

Michael was about to answer when Isabella spoke through her grief. "That night . . . that night you kicked Robbie in the driveway . . . Michael came over to help. It was the first time I had seen him since the night of the fire. I instantly recognized his face. It shocked me to see him standing here in your house. I had no idea the man I had seen in my backyard was our neighbor . . . I didn't know how to react, what to say. When I had seen him the night of the fire holding a gun, I actually thought he had shot Anthony, that maybe he had started the fire to cover up what he had done. I thought that there'd be a bullet wound, that the coroner's report would show that Anthony had been killed at someone else's hand. I had a gun, but I knew the bullet wouldn't match." She shook her head and looked up at us, her eyes scanning our faces. "It was a total surprise to me when there was no bullet wound. The paramedics had pulled Anthony out of the fire and tried to resuscitate him. I told them he had been shot, but there was no wound, nothing but his burned skin and poisoned lungs. I realized then that maybe Anthony had really been alive while I stood and watched through the windows, that I might actually have been able to save him."

Junior spoke for the first time, "Why didn't you tell the police about seeing my father? Why didn't you explain all this back then? You must have thought he started the fire."

Isabella continued to shake her head, her eyes now fixed on the kitchen table. "It got crazy really quick. The fire department came along with the police and ambulance. I told the police I had seen a man in the backyard with a gun. They interviewed the neighbors. No one heard a gunshot. No one had seen anyone there but me. They had heard me fighting with Anthony shortly before the fire broke out. The police simply didn't believe me. There was no bullet wound. There had been no gunshot. There was simply no evidence to support my story. I had never even called for help. A neighbor had seen the fire and had called it in. In the end, the story of the strange man with the gun backfired. It made me look like I was trying to cover up for what I had done."

Junior reached over and handed Isabella a napkin from the center of the table. Michael finished the story as Isabella wiped the tears from her face. "After that night with Robert, I stayed on the couch to make sure he didn't come back and bother you or Willie. Isabella came downstairs early the next morning and confronted me. We went next door to my house. That's when I explained who I was and what happened."

"Your father offered to help me," Isabella said, looking up at Junior. "We agreed to wait and see if he needed to get involved. At some point, depending on how the trial was going, he knew I might have to call him as a witness. We were both hoping that wouldn't become necessary." She sighed and rubbed at her eyes. "Part of me feels like I should pay for what happened that night. If I hadn't let my anger and self-pity get the best of me, I might have made the choice to save Anthony."

"You couldn't have saved him, Isabella," Michael said. "Before you got there, I tried to go inside that house and couldn't make it more than ten feet. You would never have been able to save him."

"But I didn't know that then. What does that say about me, that I didn't even make the effort? That I was so absorbed in my own anger and self-pity that I stood and watched my husband die from behind a pane of glass . . ." Her voice trailed off, and she dabbed at her eyes.

"I should have gone to the police right away," Michael said. "I'm ashamed that I didn't . . . but my head wasn't right then." He sat down and leaned back against the chair, taking a breath so deep that I could hear his lungs rattle. Then he shrugged and said, "But I have to make things right. It's not fair to Isabella. It's not fair to anyone."

"We can think up another story, another reason you went there," Junior said. "Maybe just say you were going to beat him up or something. You don't need to mention the gun, Dad. They don't need to know about the gun."

Michael's eyes drifted to mine. He searched my face and waited for a reaction. "Your son is right," I said. "You don't need to tell them about the gun."

Michael smiled slightly, showing his appreciation for our concern, and said, "But I do have to tell them about the gun. They're going to be skeptical of my story because I've waited so long to tell it. How else do

I explain what I did—why I didn't immediately come forward unless I also explain what it was that I feared. The gun and my intent that night explains all that. It explains that I feared being arrested. Besides, I need to corroborate Isabella's initial story, that she saw me there with a gun in my hand. I need to show them that she was telling the truth."

"But, Dad . . . they still might not believe you. And you and Isabella could both go to jail for letting a man die."

"No," I said. "I didn't learn much from Robert, but one thing I do know is that it's not against the law to choose not to save someone, not unless you were the one who put them in harm's way to begin with."

"She's right," Isabella said. "Ralph, my lawyer, has talked to me about that many times."

"Can you win this fight without my father getting involved?" Junior asked Isabella. It was a question, but there was a pleading tone in his voice.

Before she could answer, Michael interjected, "No, son. I have to fix this now. I have to make this right." Then he looked at me. "Mike told me about your conversation, about the message from Jannie. He believes in you. He trusts in what you've told him . . . If Jannie is around us as you say, she would want me to do the right thing and fix this wrong. I'd hate to think she was disappointed in me."

Chapter 39

Michael Spain did as he promised and went to the prosecutor's office the very next morning. His son went with him while Isabella and I stayed behind. When I spoke to Isabella that morning, she told me of her intent to stay alone in her house for the day, with no lights on and no answering machine, as always. She said she needed time to sort through her thoughts and her life. I respected her need for time, time to forgive Anthony, time to forgive herself, maybe even time to forgive me.

I suspect that Isabella was also worried not only for her own future but for Michael's as well. The man she had once loved and admired, the man she thought would someday father her child, had ended up ruining so many lives. Even in death, he brought about destruction, and the toll was not yet fully tallied. It was not a situation for the weakhearted, but Isabella was anything but weak. She was a survivor, and I knew that she would claw her way back to the surface somehow, someday. She would find her way, and I prayed I would be standing next to her when she did.

Before I left Isabella alone for the day, however, I returned her favor of providing me with information to help in the divorce. I gave her ammunition against Robert and his firm to assist in her case against the insurance company. Robert was a partner in the firm that was handling the insurance company's defense of Isabella's suit for recovery under Dr. Capello's life insurance policy. He also had been tangentially involved in the case based on his apparent knowledge of the facts and legal strategy. That meant that he should not have had any discussions with Isabella about the case, including Dr. Capello's death, without her attorney present. His behavior at my house that night, particularly his aggression and threatening behavior toward Isabella concerning her alleged role in her husband's death, was not only a breach of legal ethics; it could serve as a basis for disqualifying Robert's firm from serving as counsel for the insurance company. The embarrassment and potential success of a disqualification motion would give Isabella and her attorney some fodder to bring the matter to a favorable close. When I gave this information to Isabella, she smiled more brightly than she had in weeks.

As for me, I spent that next day with Willie. He too was dealing with demons, those of being the only child to estranged parents, and I needed to show him just how much he was loved. I had underestimated the difficulties he would have with the impending divorce.

So I took him on a hike up the side of Gray's Hill, up a steadily inclining trail that found its way to a glorious view of the valley and the city below. It took us over an hour to reach the summit, and we were both sweaty and dirty when our boots finally hit flat ground, but it was a sight to behold at the top.

"This is more of a mountain than a hill," he said as we sat on one of the picnic benches that had been placed on a grassy knoll at the top.

"You've got that right," I said, wiping the sweat off my forehead and swigging down the rest of the liquid in my water bottle. "Whoever called it a hill must have been in great shape."

"I bet Mrs. Spain didn't even see this much when she sat on her roof," he said, turning to offer me a smile.

I leaned over and kissed his reddened cheek. "I'm sure she has a pretty good view, wherever she is," I said. Willie now knew that Jannie had passed away and that the two of us alone had been blessed by her spiritual presence. It was a truth he accepted more easily than I could ever have imagined, and he took pride in the special bond the experience had created between us.

"I had a dream about her," Willie said, jumping off the picnic table and grabbing a rock. He threw it against one of the large trees on the outer circle of grass.

"What was it about?"

He bent over and grabbed another rock. With his arm pulled way back, he slung it forward and watched as it bounced off a few pines and lost its way in the woods. Then he turned to me and said, "She told me to say thank you."

"For what?" I asked.

"For helping Mr. Spain. She said she could go now, that she wouldn't be visiting us anymore."

"She said that?"

"Yup. She seemed happy though."

"Did she say anything else?"

"She said that we'd be happy too, just like she was."

"What do you think she meant by that?" I asked.

He tilted his head and mentally recalled the dream. Squinting as only a six-year-old can do, the freckles on his nose glistening in the sun, he said, "Something about you not having to look out the windows anymore. What did she mean, Mom?"

I smiled and gave him a big hug. His hair was wet and sticky and smelled of a mix of sweat and that morning's shampoo. I could feel his heart beating softly inside his chest as I pulled him closer. His scent and his touch, the sound of his breath as it slowly went in and out of his mouth, reminded me of the fragility and sacredness of life. I leaned over and whispered in his ear, "I think she meant that when we are at peace with ourselves and our lives, we don't need to look out any windows to find happiness."

Willie shrugged as if he understood what I had said and went back to innocently throwing rocks against the hardwoods. I knew he would not fully comprehend his dream or Jannie's message until he was much older, until he inevitably discovered that loneliness and heartache eventually find us all and make our hearts mistakenly search for happiness outside our own skin and the false walls we hide behind. Hopefully, he would also learn, as I eventually did, that we can find ourselves again, that we can learn to love—even like—who we are and what we have become so that a state of happiness is our first instinct rather than an unexpected occurrence.

Epilogue

It took two more months before the prosecutor's office finally agreed to drop the charges against Isabella. When Michael first spoke to the lead attorney, he initially doubted the story. But Michael's clean history and reputation at the local college gave him credence; over time, even the skeptical lawyers had to concede defeat. They didn't necessarily believe in Isabella's innocence, but the evidence in her favor—including a well-spoken professor who could confirm both Isabella's initial story that there had been a man in the yard with a gun as well as the findings of her expert as to the cause and source of the fire—meant a conviction would be very difficult.

It wasn't long before the insurance company reached a settlement with Isabella as well, leaving her in a good enough financial position that she actually began to pay rent to Officer Lucarelli in order to stay in the house on Wooster Street, which she had grown to love. She still did not have an answering machine, but that was something I had learned to live with long ago. She was still speaking to me—and still coming over for an occasional glass of wine—and that was good enough for me.

As for Michael, the state did not press any charges although he was forced to surrender the gun that he had brought to the Capellos' home that fateful night. He was still living next to me on Wooster Street, but our relationship was changing. We spoke on a daily basis and had learned how much we enjoyed each other's company, even just the pleasure of watching a late movie in silence from the comfort of his couch. Sometimes we even let Willie join us although he usually fell asleep without making it to the end of the movie.

Thankfully, Robert had come to his senses or, at least, had been forced to his senses by his own indiscretions. There was only one thing Robert wanted more than revenge against Isabella, and that was his partnership at the firm. So he avoided a nasty divorce proceeding that was certain to highlight his extramarital activities with a junior lawyer's wife and eventually conceded to my demands, negotiating for an extra week with Willie in the summer just to save face.

I haven't seen Jannie again, nor have I had any more dreams, but I think of her often. The image of her smiling face and gentle voice is always with me. Her memory brings me hope. It brings me joy. For now I know that no matter how difficult and unbearable life can become, no matter how unfair it may seem at times, the line of life is not meant to be an easy line to travel. It is meant to twist and turn and suddenly drop off. It is only by enduring the unexpected interruptions and the painful dips that we can truly appreciate the flat terrain when it comes. It is only by losing something or someone, maybe even ourselves for a time, that we learn to treasure what we are and what we still have.

I also now know, with a certainty I never before enjoyed, that life does not end with the suddenness of a dot at the end of an obituary. There is a bend in the line that temporarily pulls us out of earthly view until those we leave behind turn the corner and see for themselves the wonder and beauty of our boundless existence, an existence with a beautiful view and no thoughts of looking through windows for something better on the other side.